Dear parents, caregivers, and educators:

If you want to get your child excited about reading, you've come to the right place! Ready-to-Read *GRAPHICS* is the perfect launchpad for emerging graphic novel readers.

All Ready-to-Read *GRAPHICS* books include the following:

★ **A how-to guide to reading graphic novels for first-time readers**

★ **Easy-to-follow panels to support reading comprehension**

★ **Accessible vocabulary to build your child's reading confidence**

★ **Compelling stories that star your child's favorite characters**

★ **Fresh, engaging illustrations that provide context and promote visual literacy**

Wherever your child may be on their reading journey, Ready-to-Read *GRAPHICS* will make them giggle, gasp, and want to keep reading more.

Blast off on this starry adventure . . . a universe of graphic novel reading awaits!

NUGGET AND DOG

S'MORE THAN MEETS THE EYE!

written and illustrated by
JASON THARP

Ready-to-Read GRAPHICS

SIMON SPOTLIGHT

An imprint of Simon & Schuster Children's Publishing Division • New York • London • Toronto • Sydney • New Delhi
1230 Avenue of the Americas, New York, New York 10020 • This Simon Spotlight edition May 2022
Text and illustrations copyright © 2022 by Jason Tharp • All rights reserved, including the right of reproduction in whole or in part in any form.
SIMON SPOTLIGHT, READY-TO-READ, and colophon are registered trademarks of Simon & Schuster, Inc. For information about special discounts for bulk purchases,
please contact Simon & Schuster Special Sales at 1-866-506-1949 or business@simonandschuster.com. Manufactured in the United States of America 0322 LAK
1 2 3 4 5 6 7 8 9 10 • This book has been cataloged by the Library of Congress.
ISBN 978-1-6659-1329-4 (hc) • ISBN 978-1-6659-1328-7 (pbk) • ISBN 978-1-6659-1330-0 (ebook)

You can be a K.E.T.C.H.U.P. Crusader anytime, remember it's:

Kind
Empathetic
Thoughtful
Courageous
Helpful
Unique
Powerful

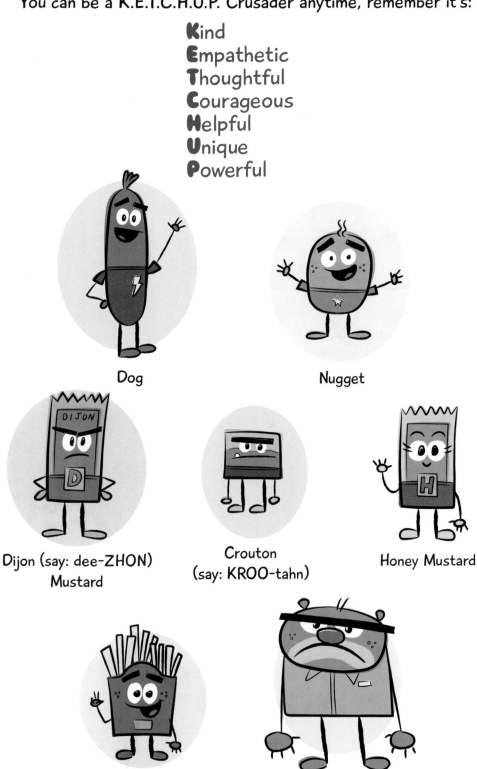

Dog

Nugget

Dijon (say: dee-ZHON)
Mustard

Crouton
(say: KROO-tahn)

Honey Mustard

Fry

Grizzle

CONTENTS

How to Read This Book

This is Dog. He is here to give you some tips on how to read this book.

If there is a box like this one, read the words inside the box first. Then read the words in the speech or thought bubbles below it...

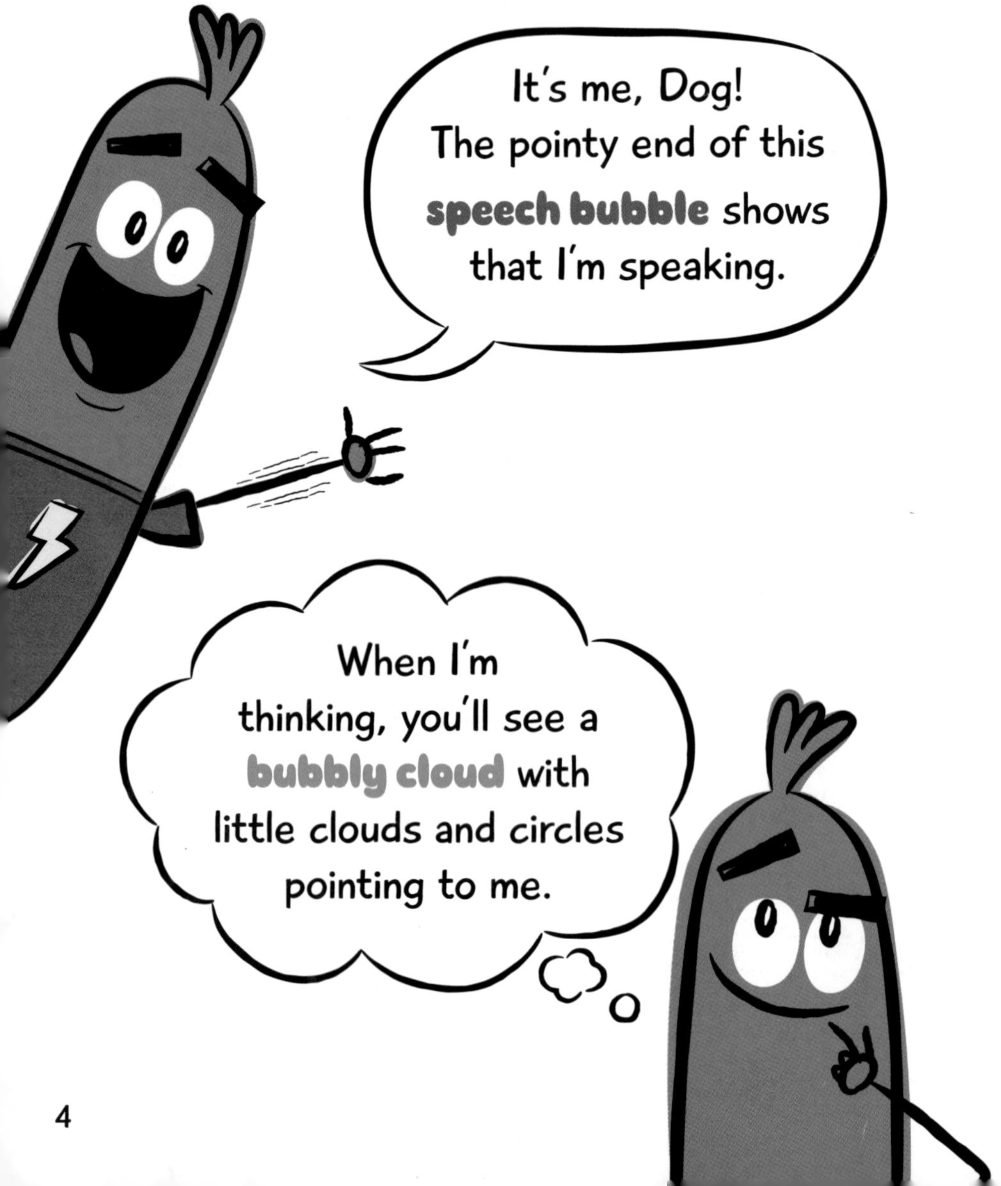
It's me, Dog!
The pointy end of this **speech bubble** shows that I'm speaking.
When I'm thinking, you'll see a **bubbly cloud** with little clouds and circles pointing to me.

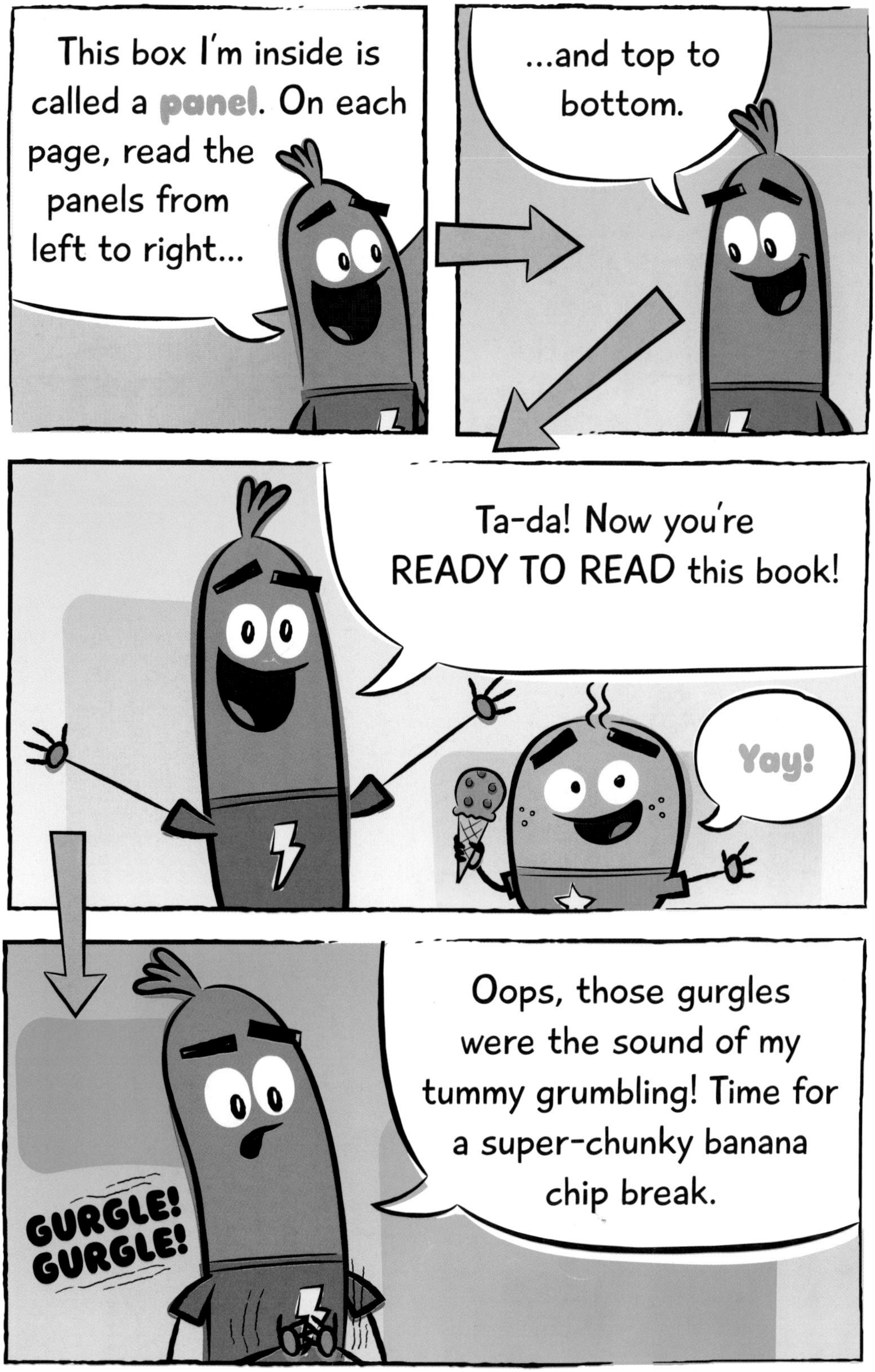
This box I'm inside is called a panel. On each page, read the panels from left to right...
...and top to bottom.
Ta-da! Now you're READY TO READ this book!
Yay!
GURGLE! GURGLE!
Oops, those gurgles were the sound of my tummy grumbling! Time for a super-chunky banana chip break.

Chapter 1

K.E.T.C.H.U.P. WITH US!

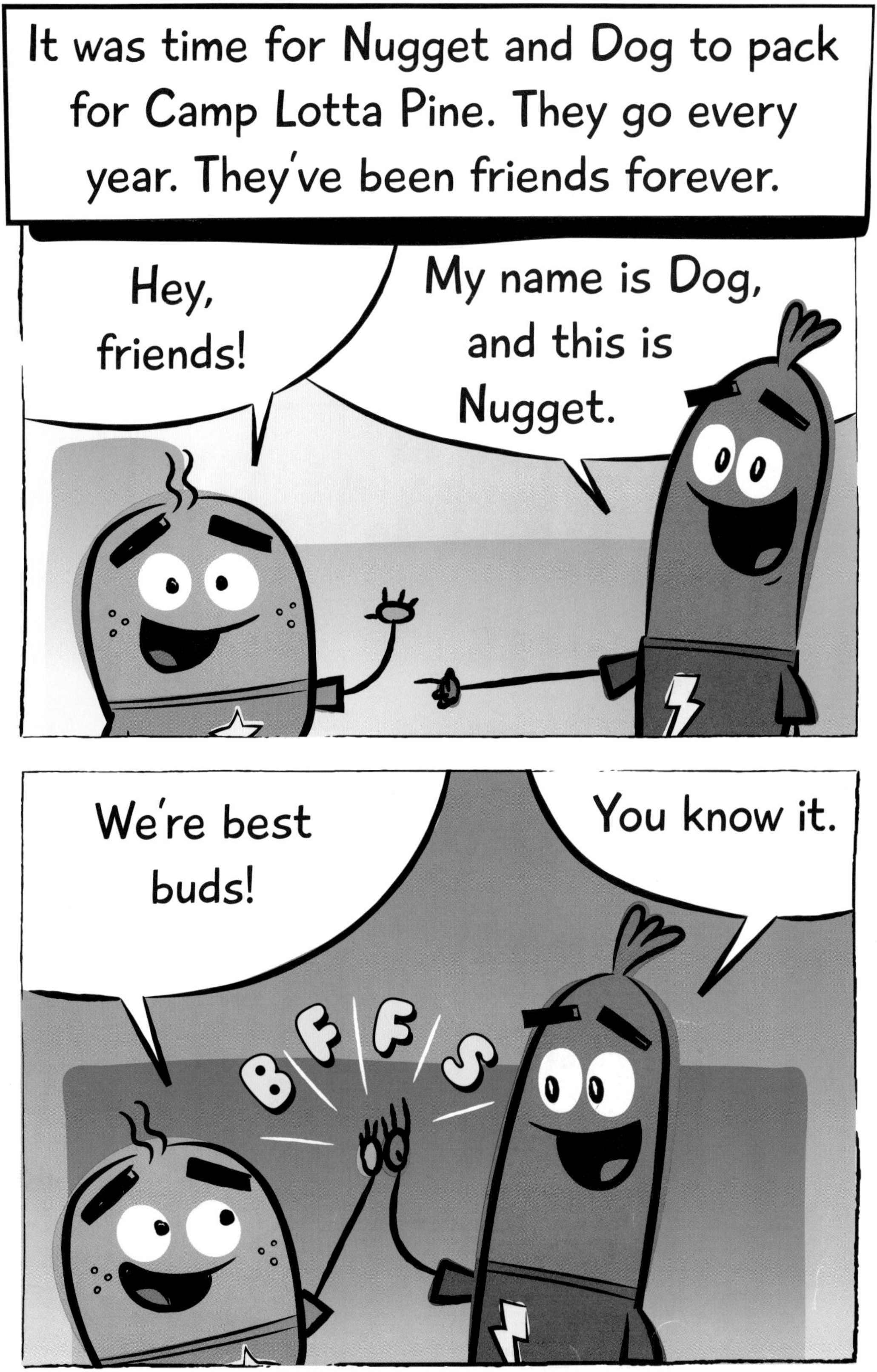
It was time for Nugget and Dog to pack for Camp Lotta Pine. They go every year. They've been friends forever.
Hey, friends!
My name is Dog, and this is Nugget.
We're best buds!
You know it.
BFFS

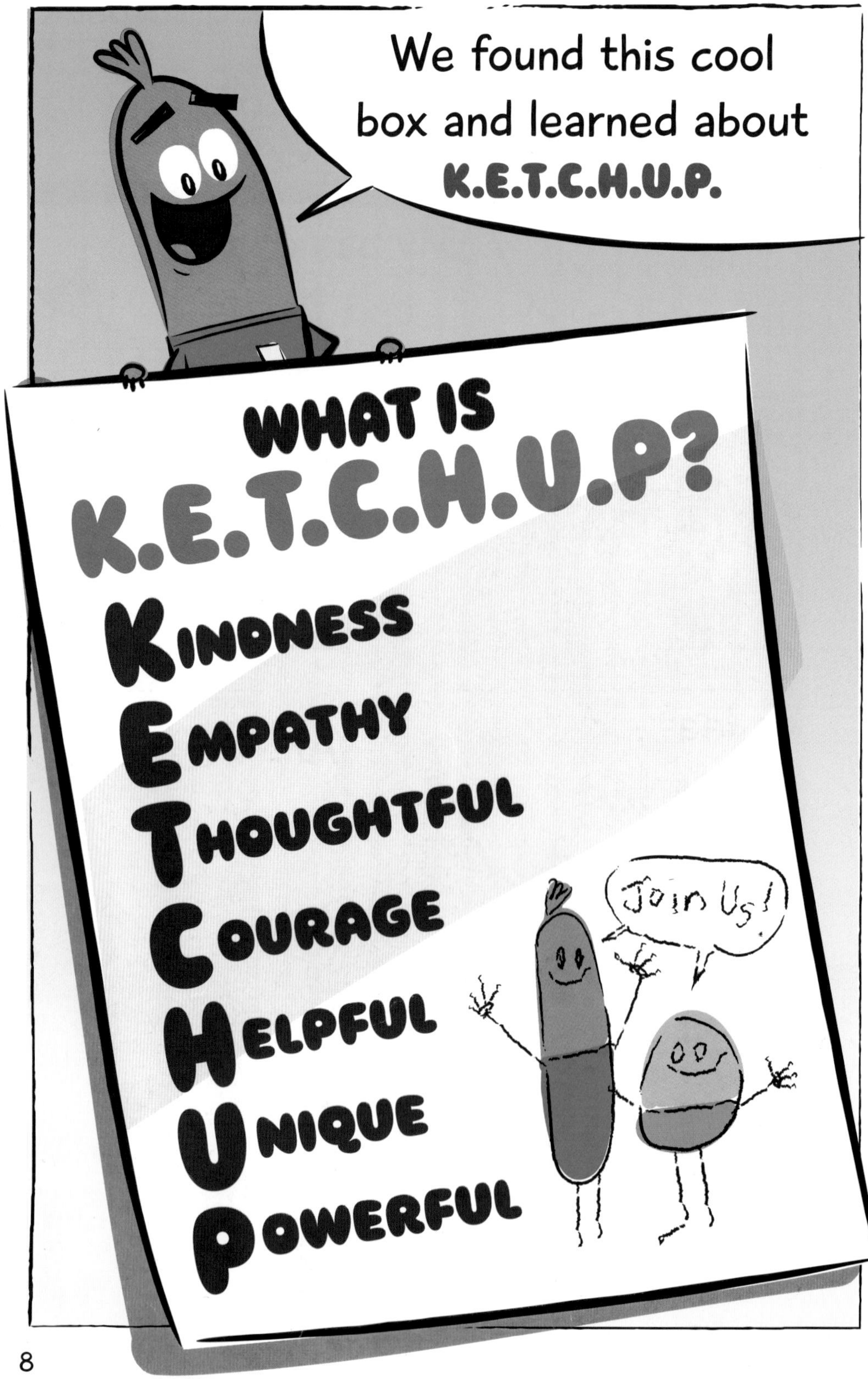
We found this cool box and learned about K.E.T.C.H.U.P.
WHAT IS K.E.T.C.H.U.P?
KINDNESS
EMPATHY
THOUGHTFUL
COURAGE
HELPFUL
UNIQUE
POWERFUL
Join Us!

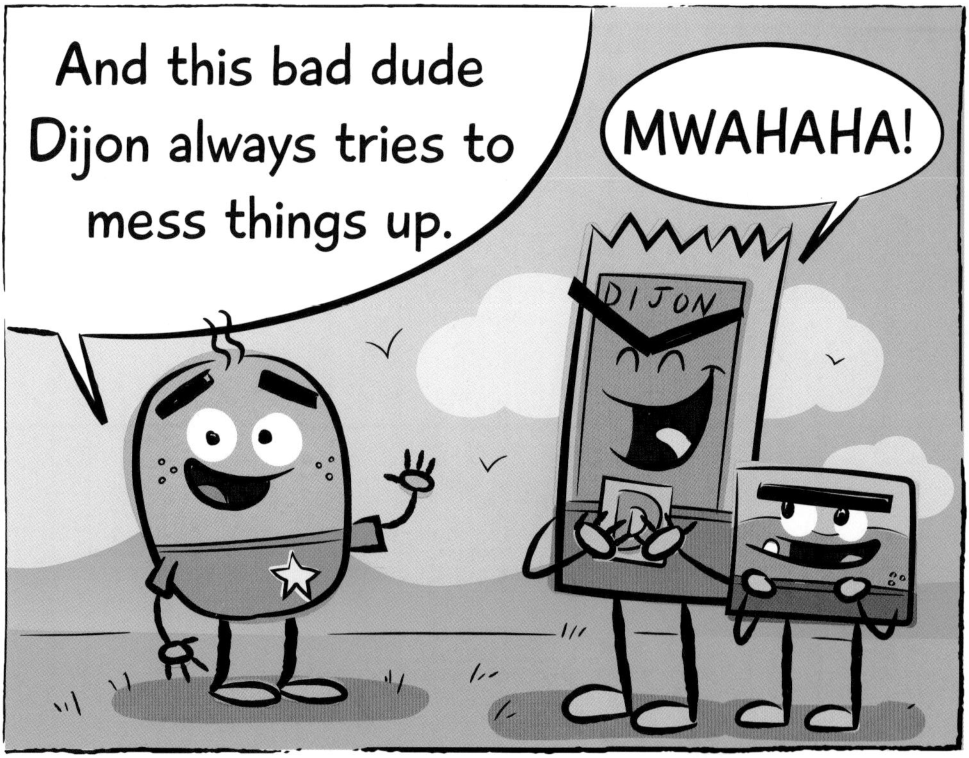
And this bad dude Dijon always tries to mess things up.
MWAHAHA!
DIJON

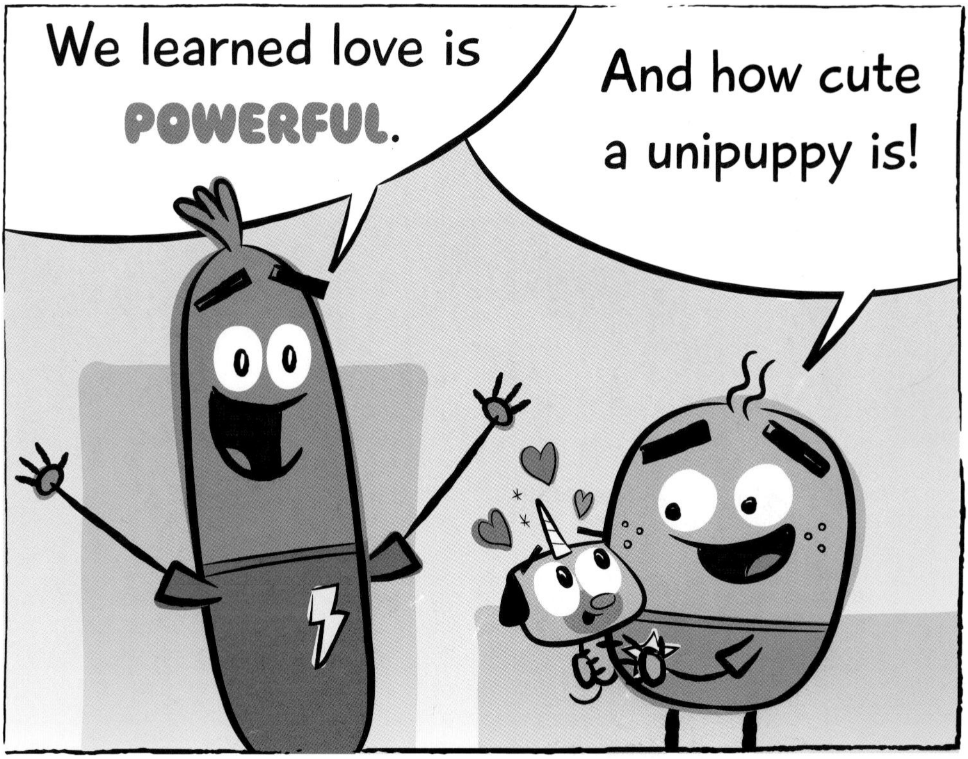
We learned love is POWERFUL.
And how cute a unipuppy is!

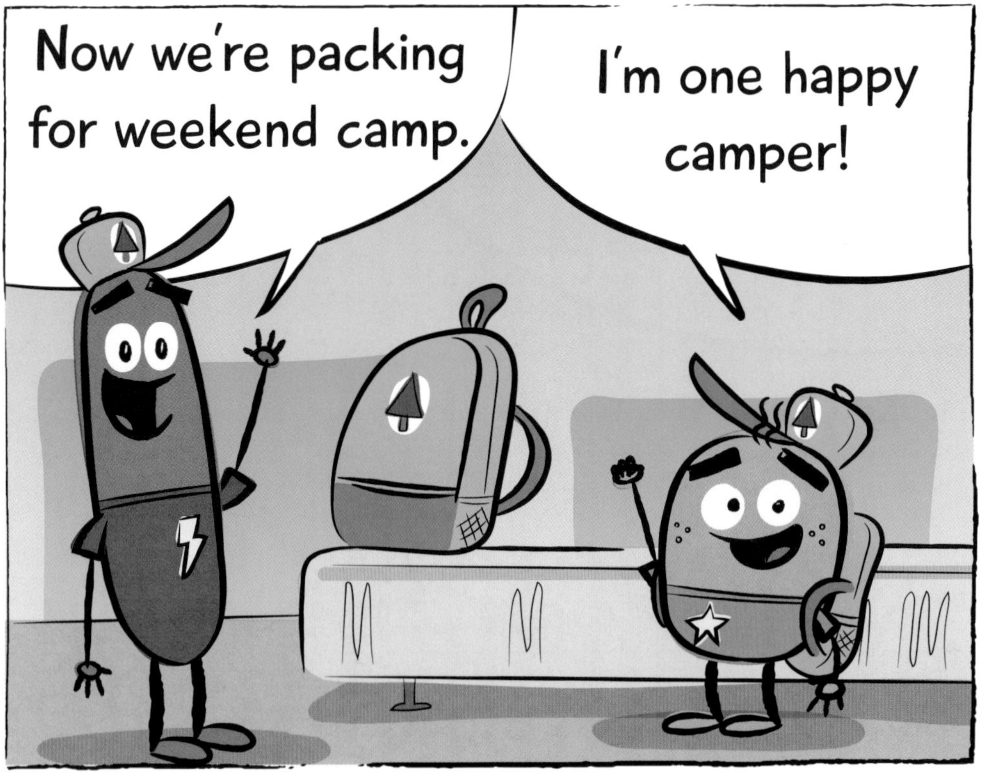
Now we're packing for weekend camp.
I'm one happy camper!

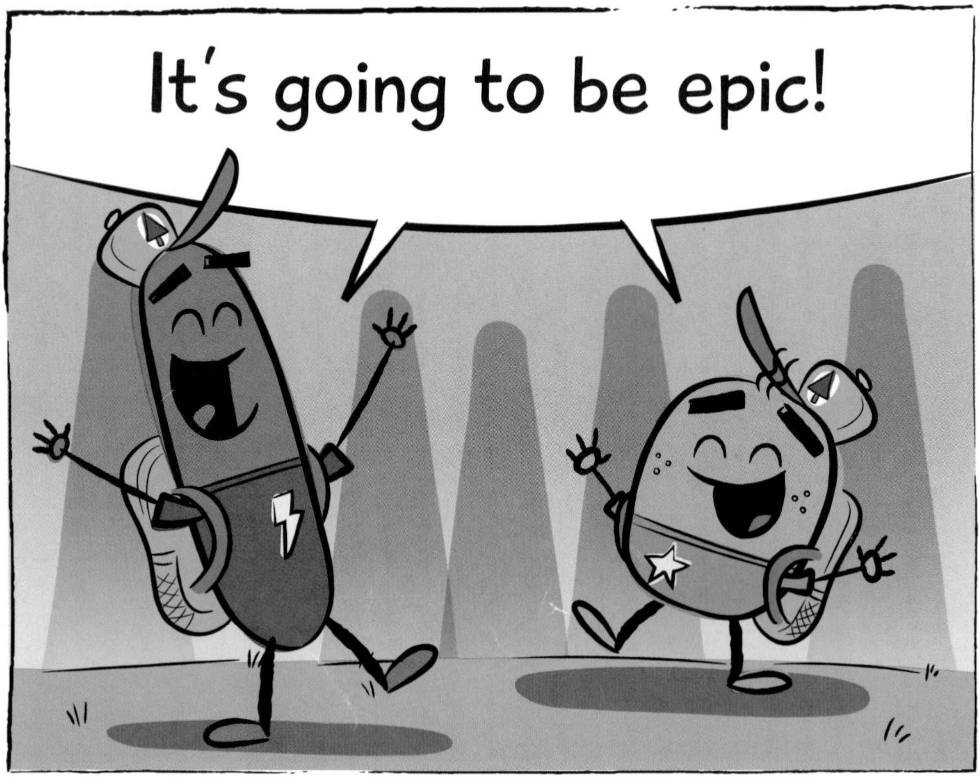
It's going to be epic!

Chapter 2

WELCOME TO CAMP LOTTA PINE!

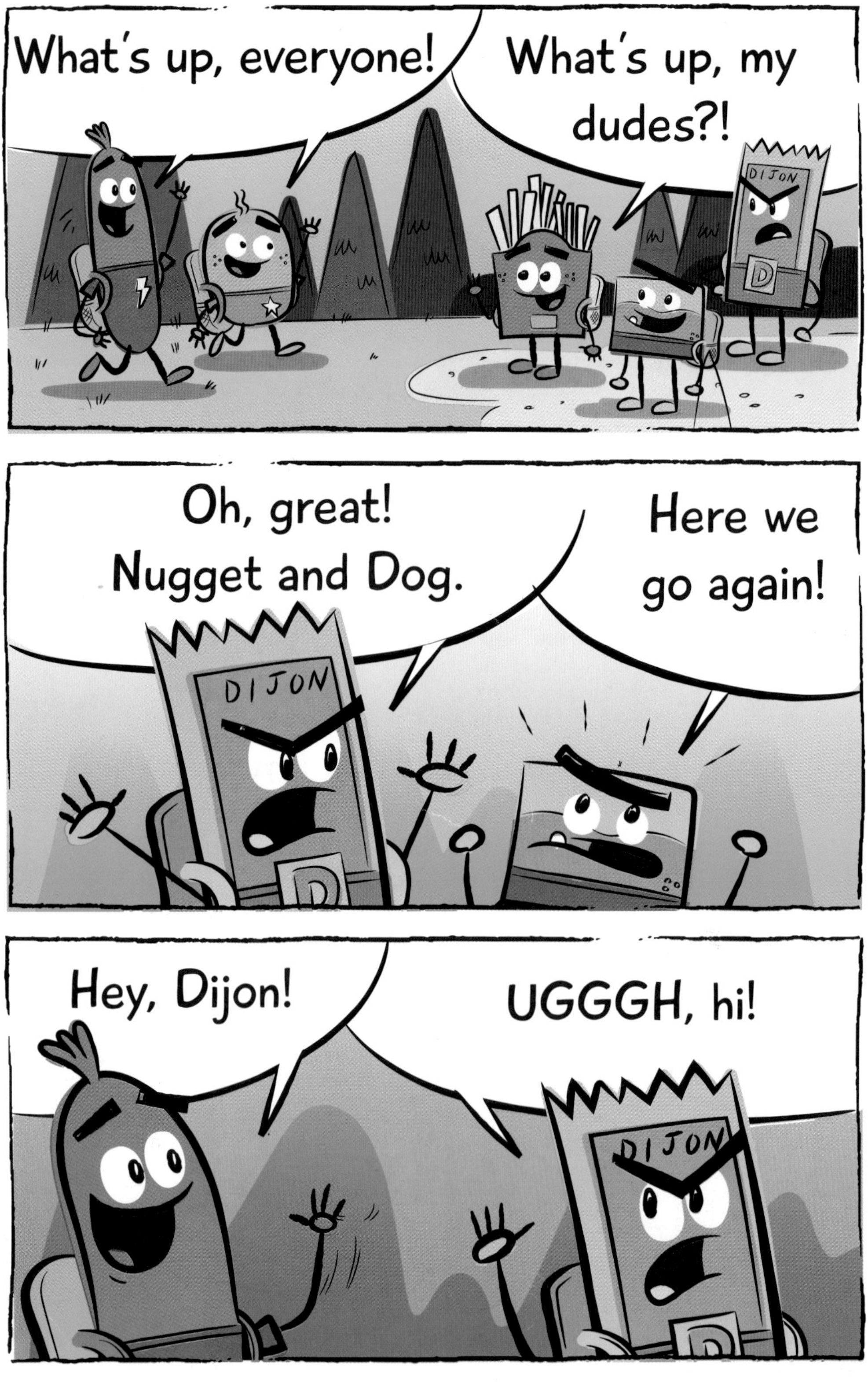
What's up, everyone!
What's up, my dudes?!
DIJON
Oh, great! Nugget and Dog.
Here we go again!
DIJON
Hey, Dijon!
UGGGH, hi!
DIJON

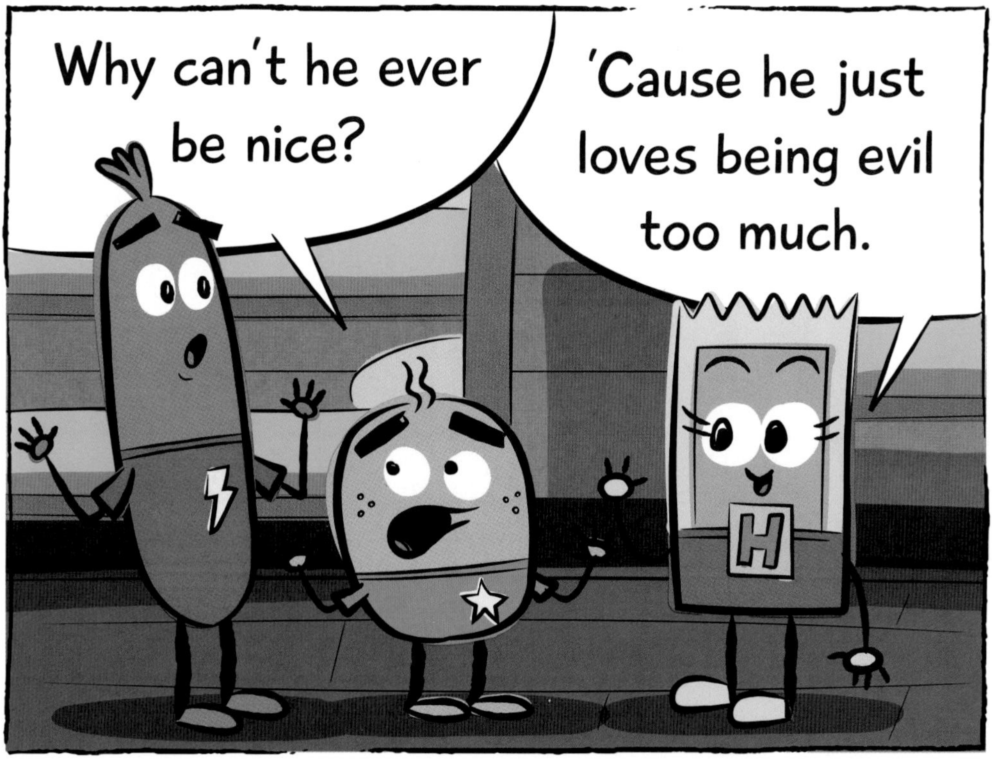
Why can't he ever be nice?
'Cause he just loves being evil too much.

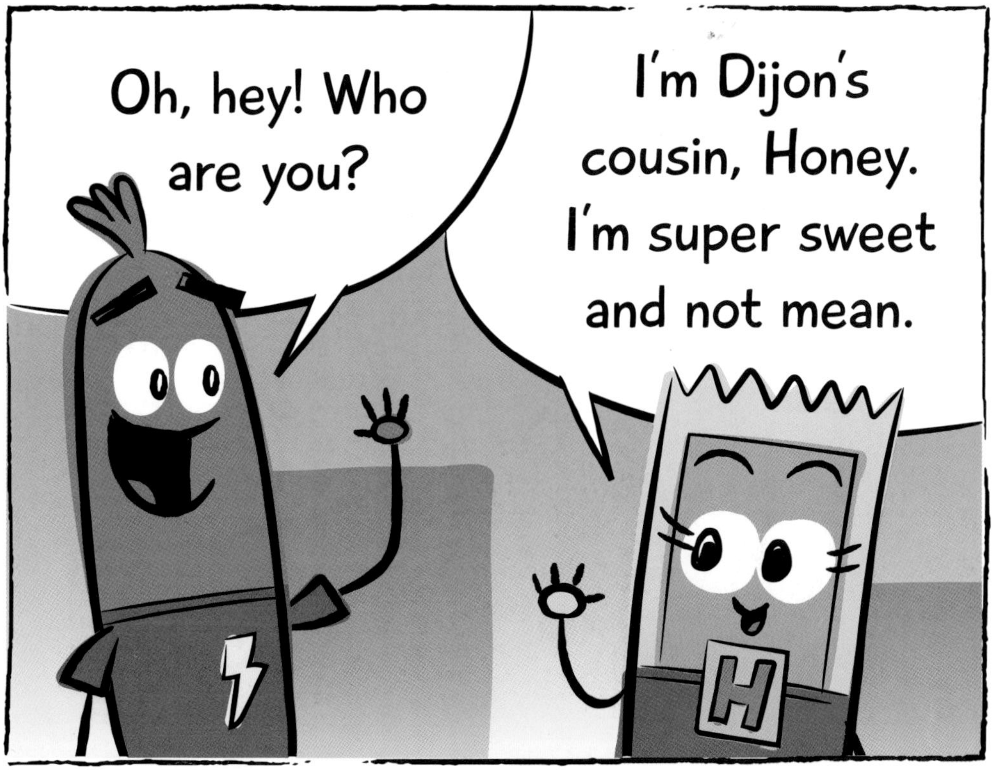
Oh, hey! Who are you?
I'm Dijon's cousin, Honey. I'm super sweet and not mean.

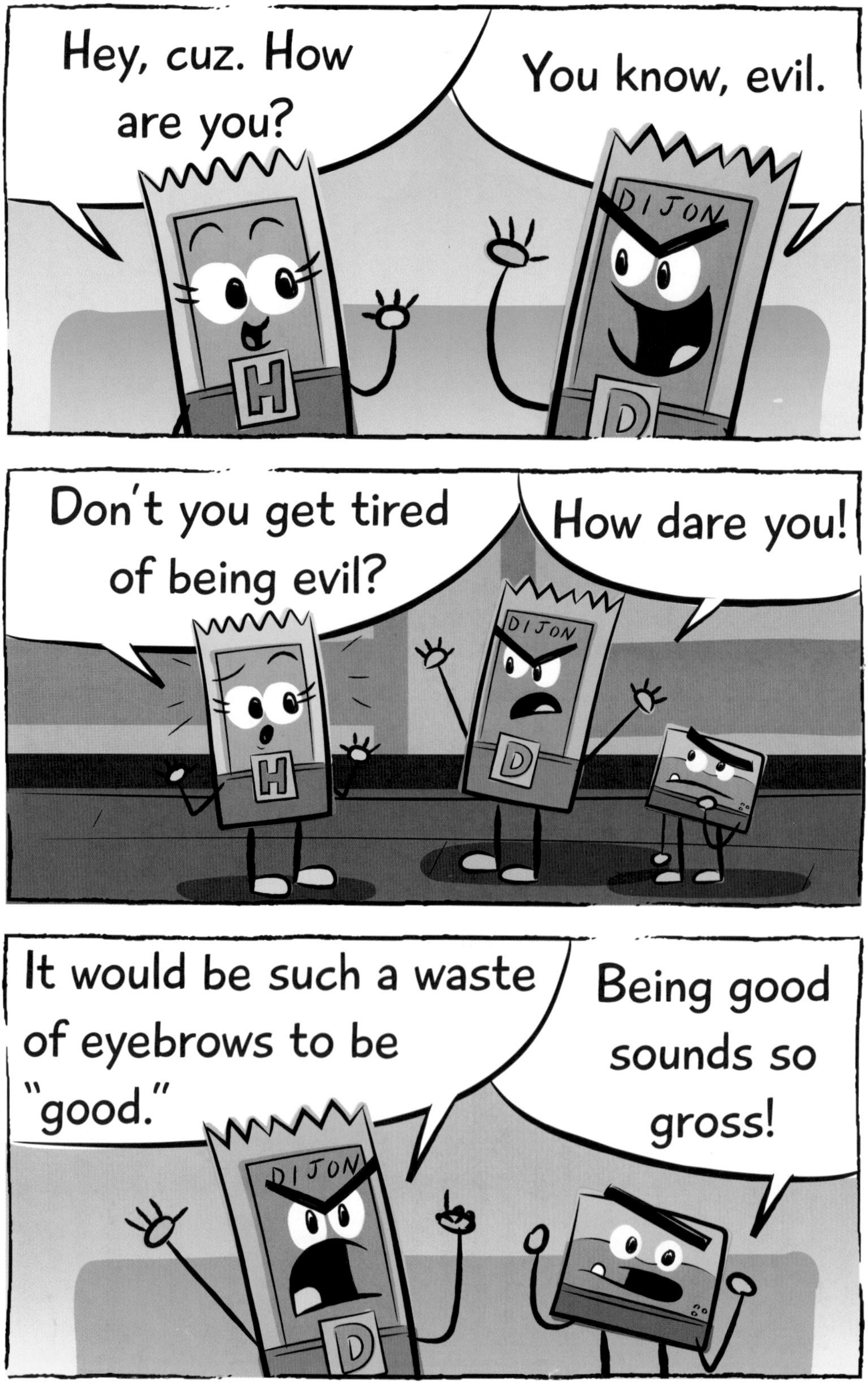
Hey, cuz. How are you?
You know, evil.
DIJON
H
D
Don't you get tired of being evil?
How dare you!
It would be such a waste of eyebrows to be "good."
Being good sounds so gross!

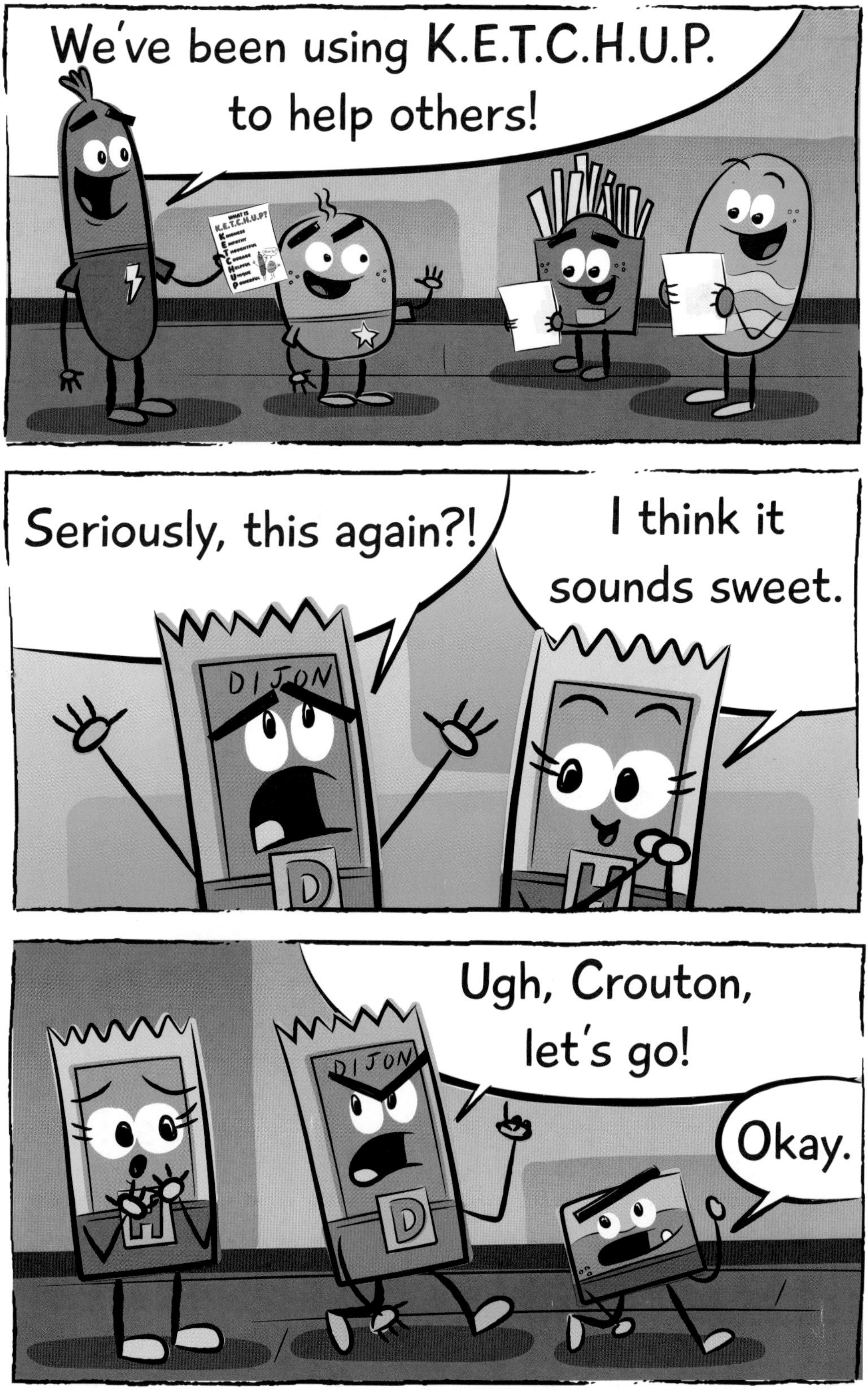
We've been using K.E.T.C.H.U.P. to help others!
Seriously, this again?!
DIJON
I think it sounds sweet.
DIJON
Ugh, Crouton, let's go!
Okay.

Chapter 3

NAME THE CABIN

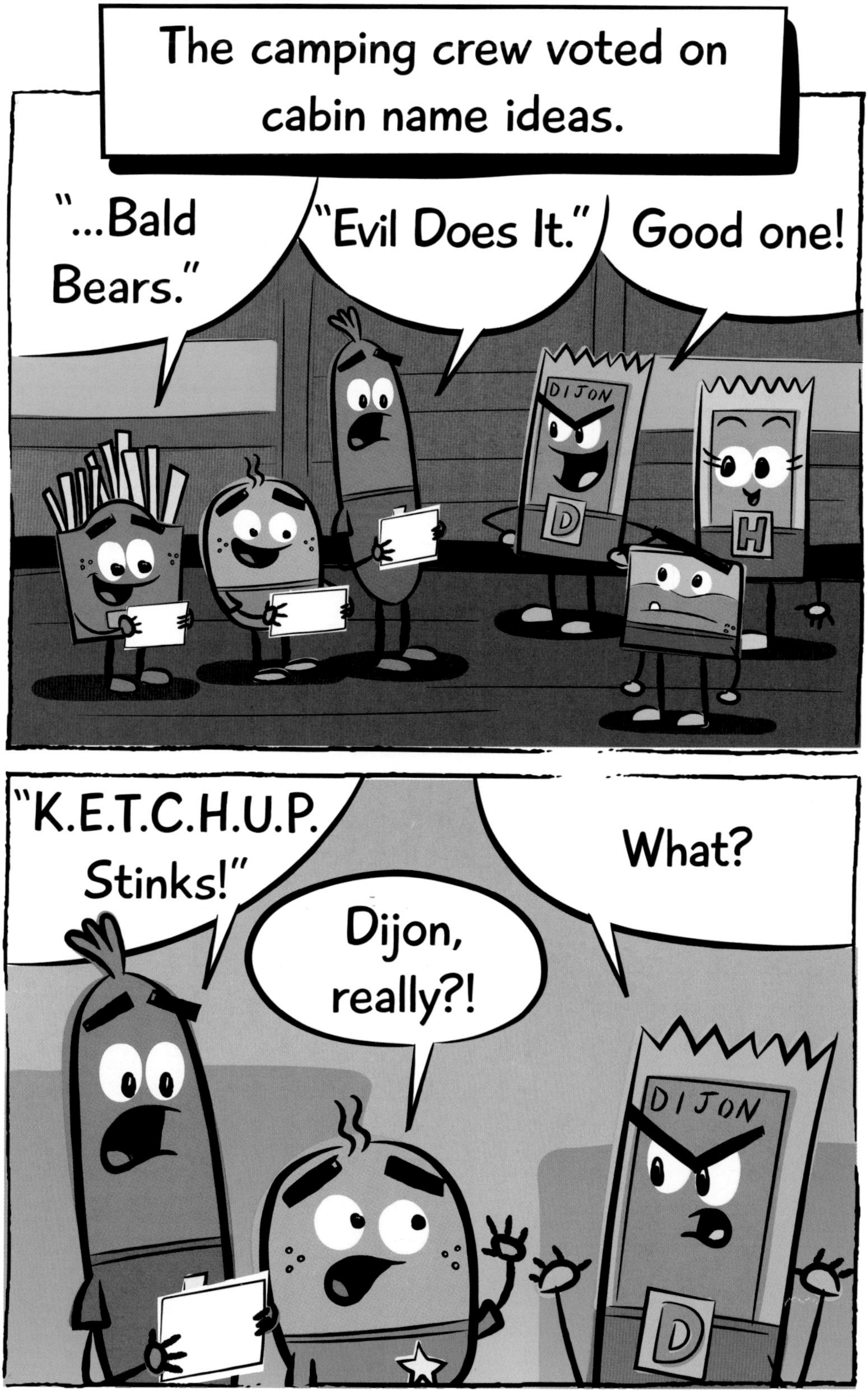
The camping crew voted on cabin name ideas.
"...Bald Bears."
"Evil Does It."
Good one!
"K.E.T.C.H.U.P. Stinks!"
Dijon, really?!
What?

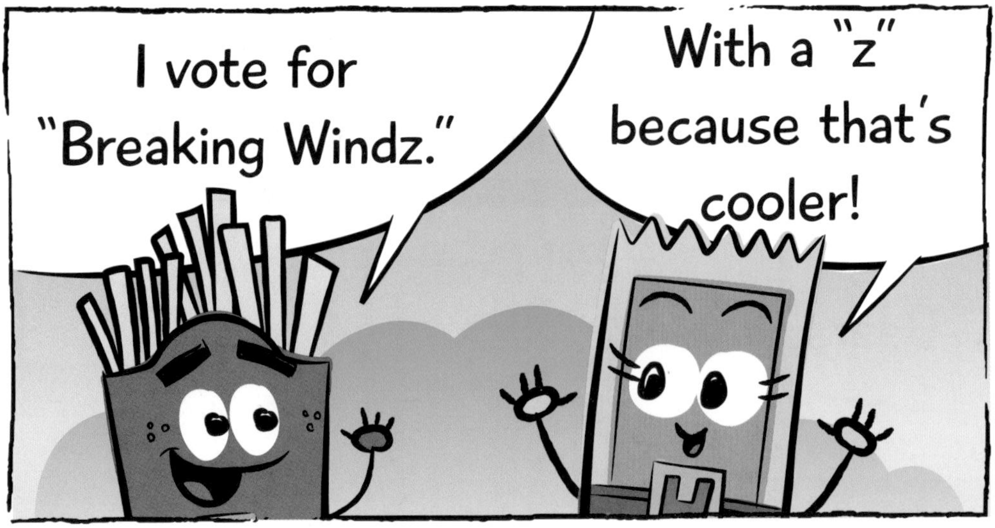
I vote for "Breaking Windz."
With a "z" because that's cooler!

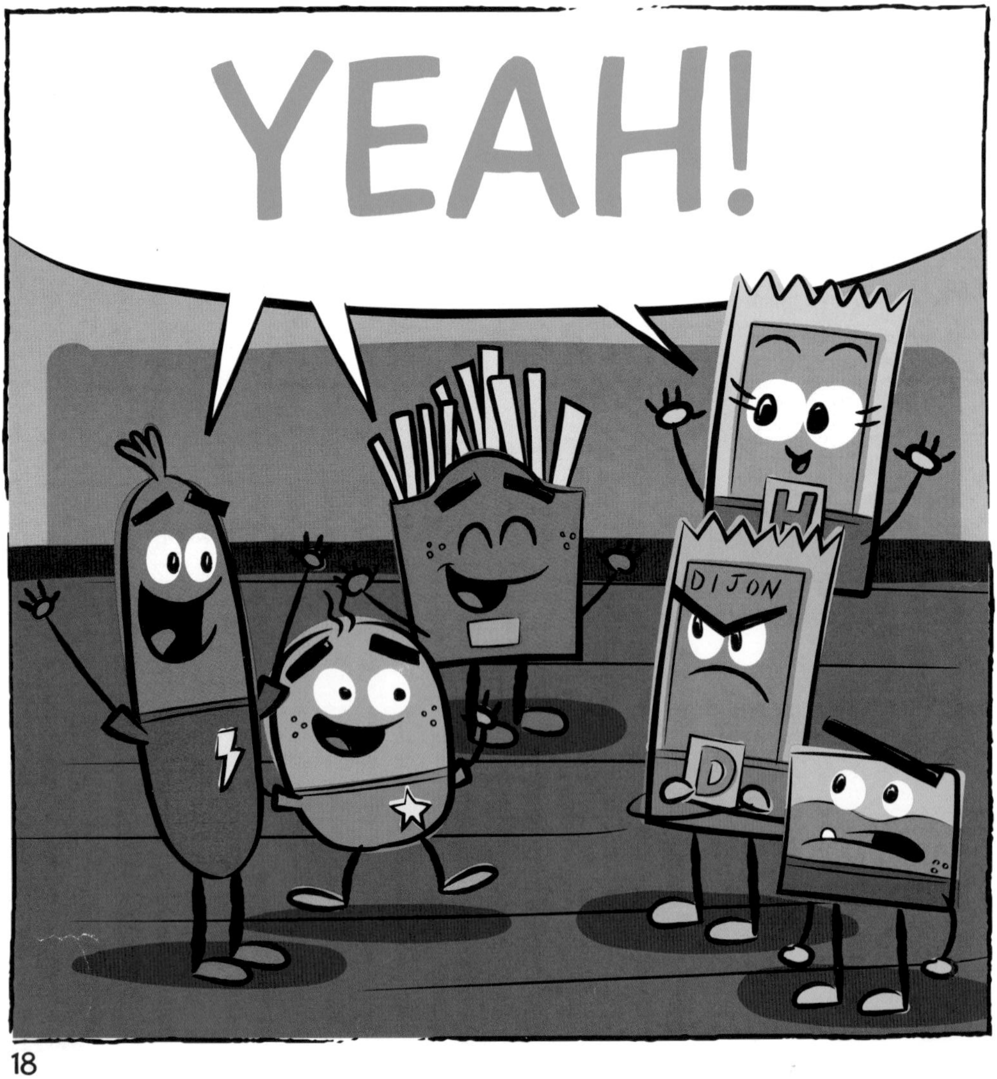
YEAH!
DIJON

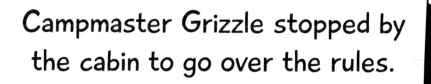

Campmaster Grizzle stopped by the cabin to go over the rules.

The rules for camp are simple. One, keep fun to a minimum. Two, stay out of my way. Three, remember to stay out of my way!

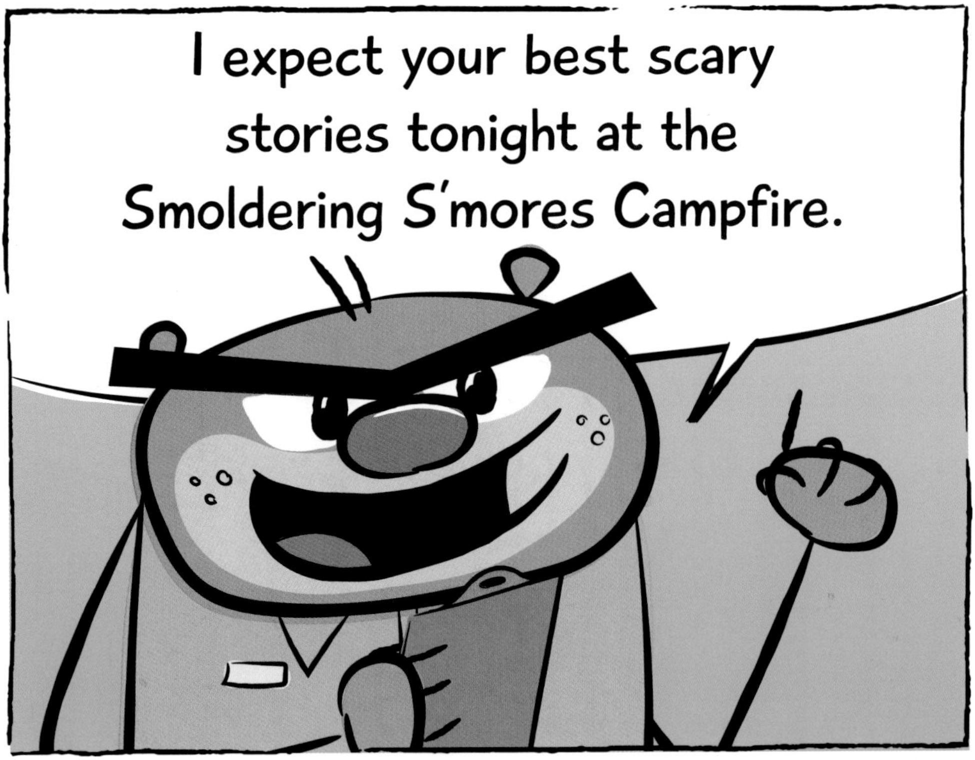
I expect your best scary stories tonight at the Smoldering S'mores Campfire.

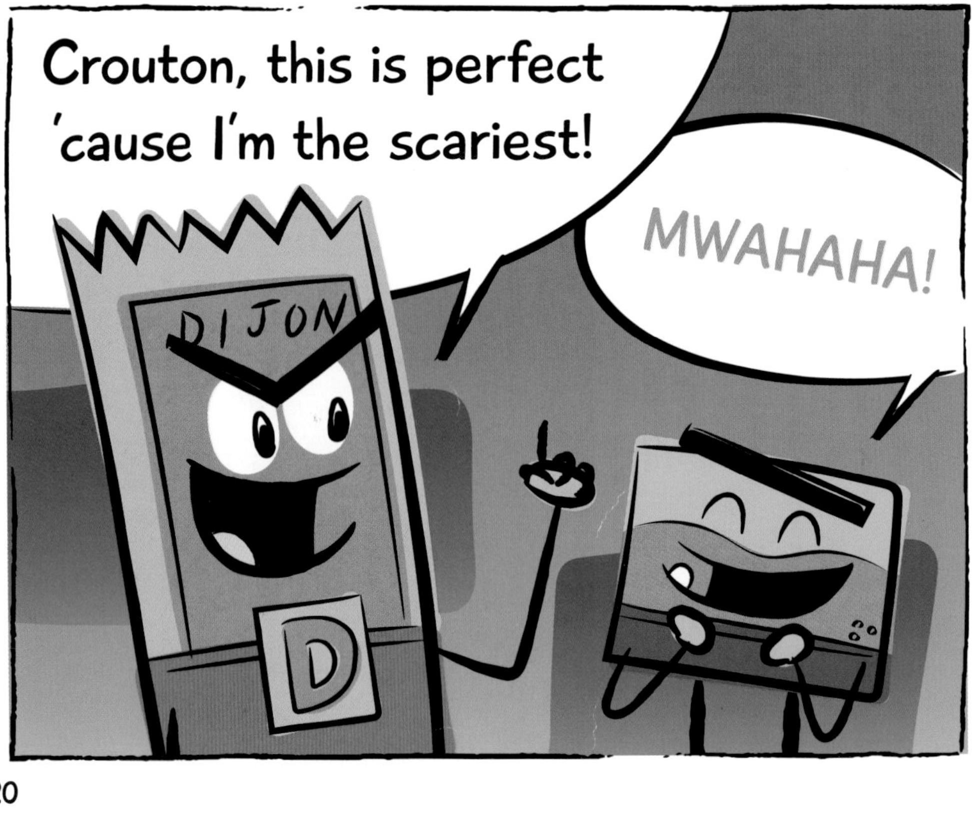
Crouton, this is perfect 'cause I'm the scariest!
MWAHAHA!
DIJON
D

Chapter 4

I DON'T SCARE!

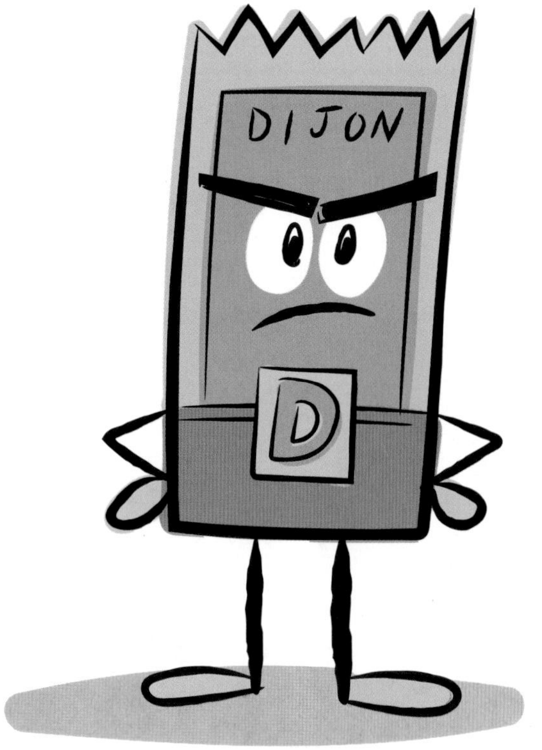
DIJON
D

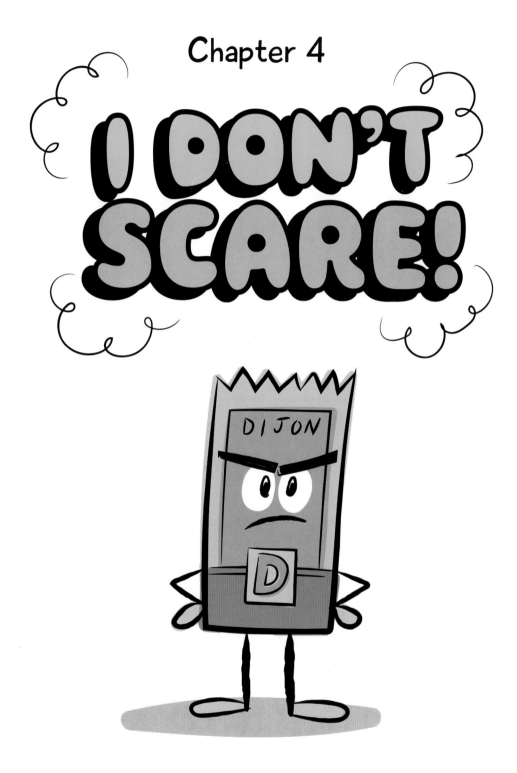

Dijon and Crouton spent the rest of the day planning the ultimate scary story.

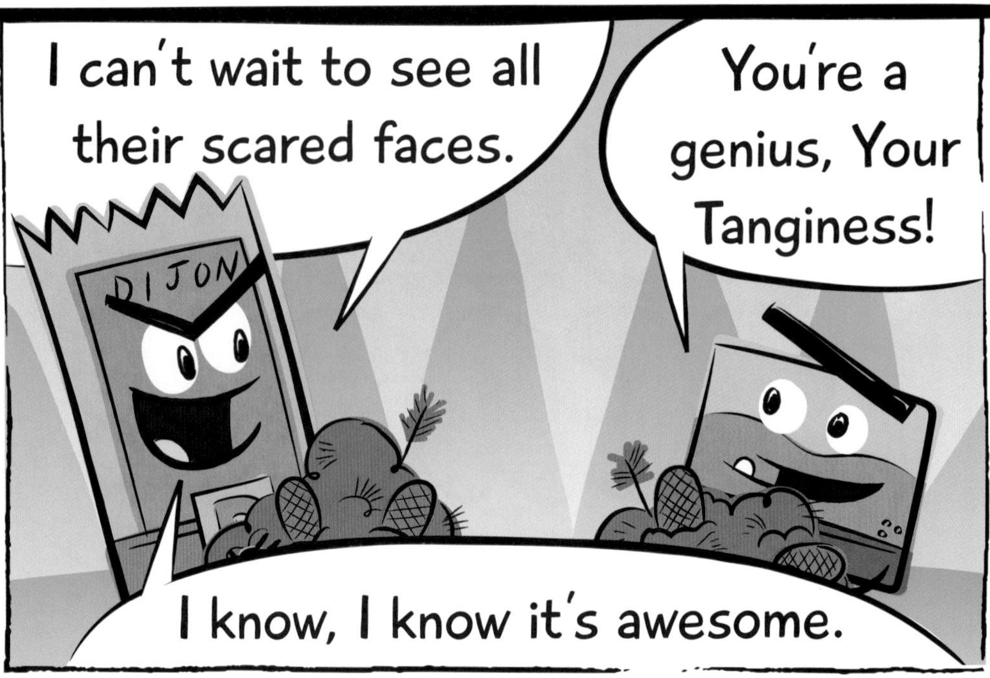
I can't wait to see all their scared faces.
You're a genius, Your Tanginess!
DIJON
I know, I know it's awesome.

Soon all the campers were gathered around the campfire, and Honey Mustard began her story.

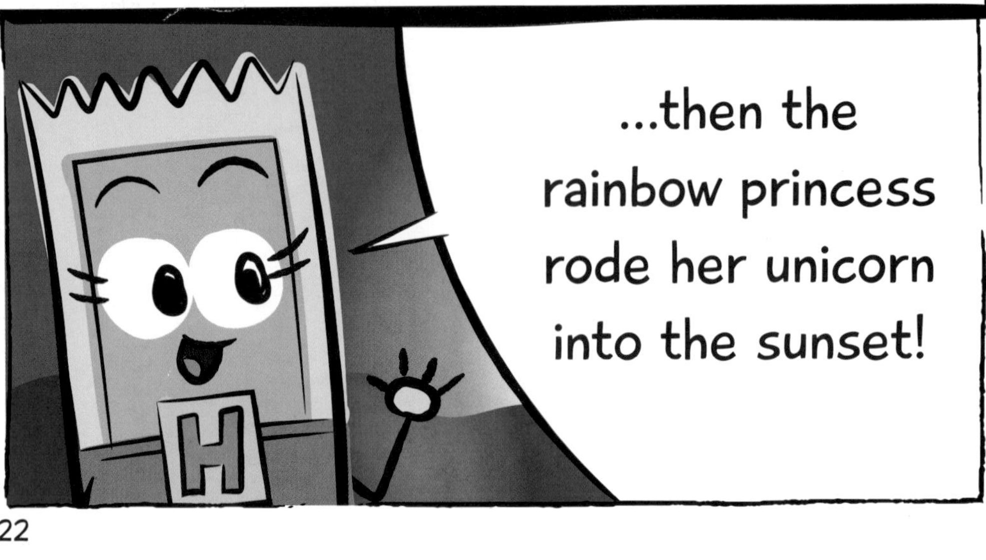
...then the rainbow princess rode her unicorn into the sunset!
H

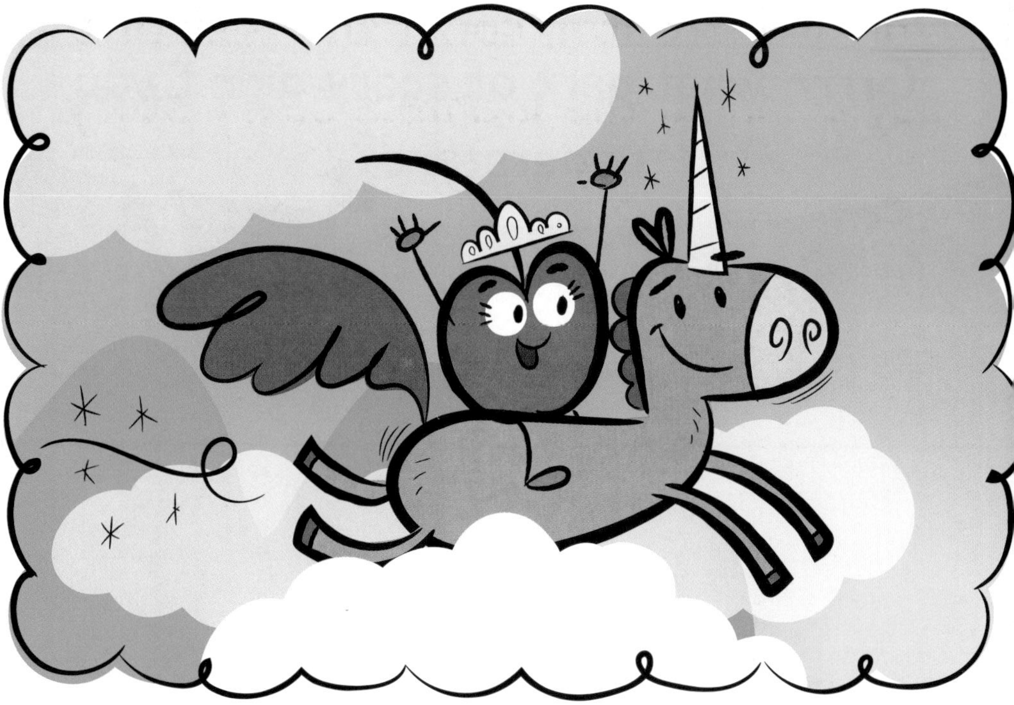

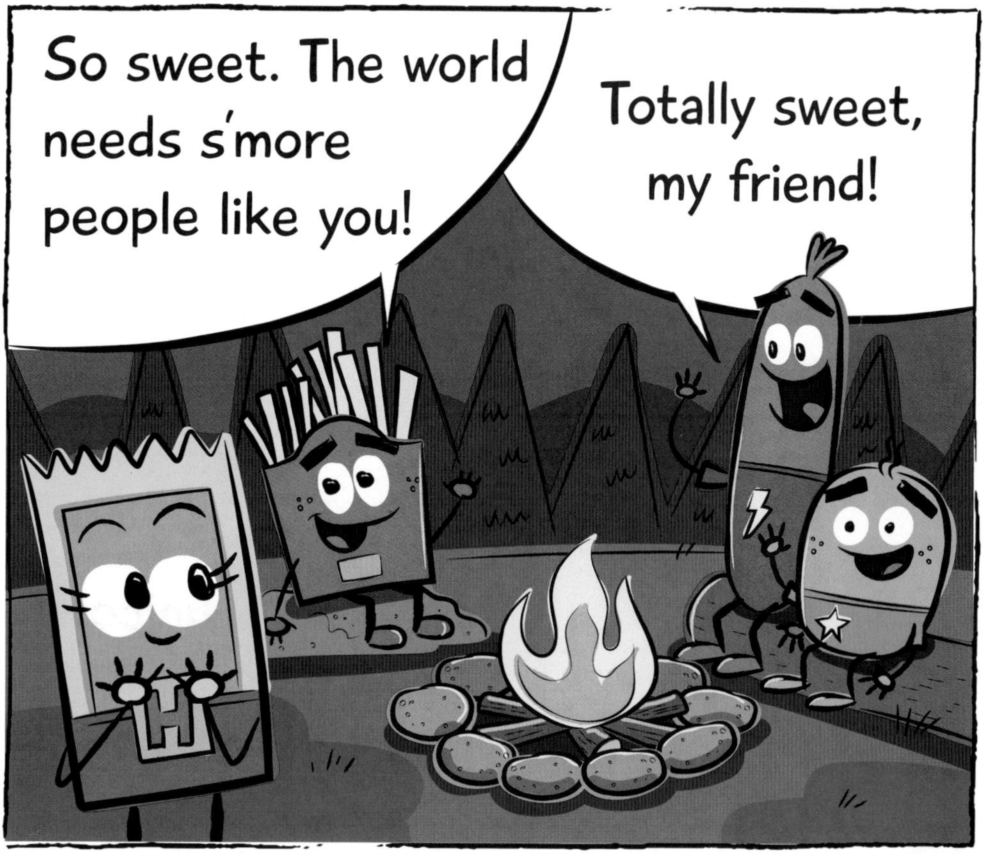
So sweet. The world needs s'more people like you!
Totally sweet, my friend!

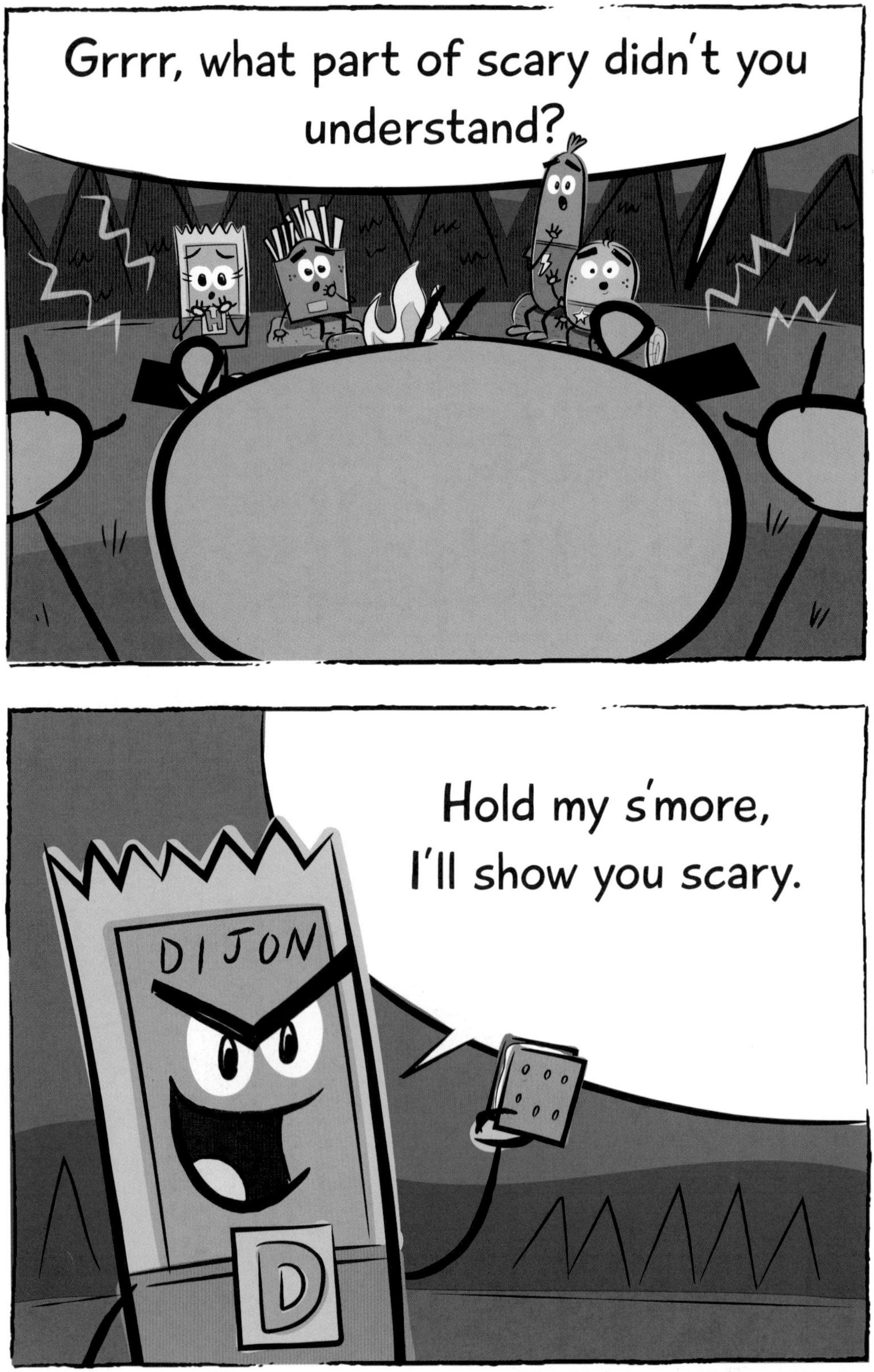
Grrrr, what part of scary didn't you understand?
Hold my s'more, I'll show you scary.
DIJON
D

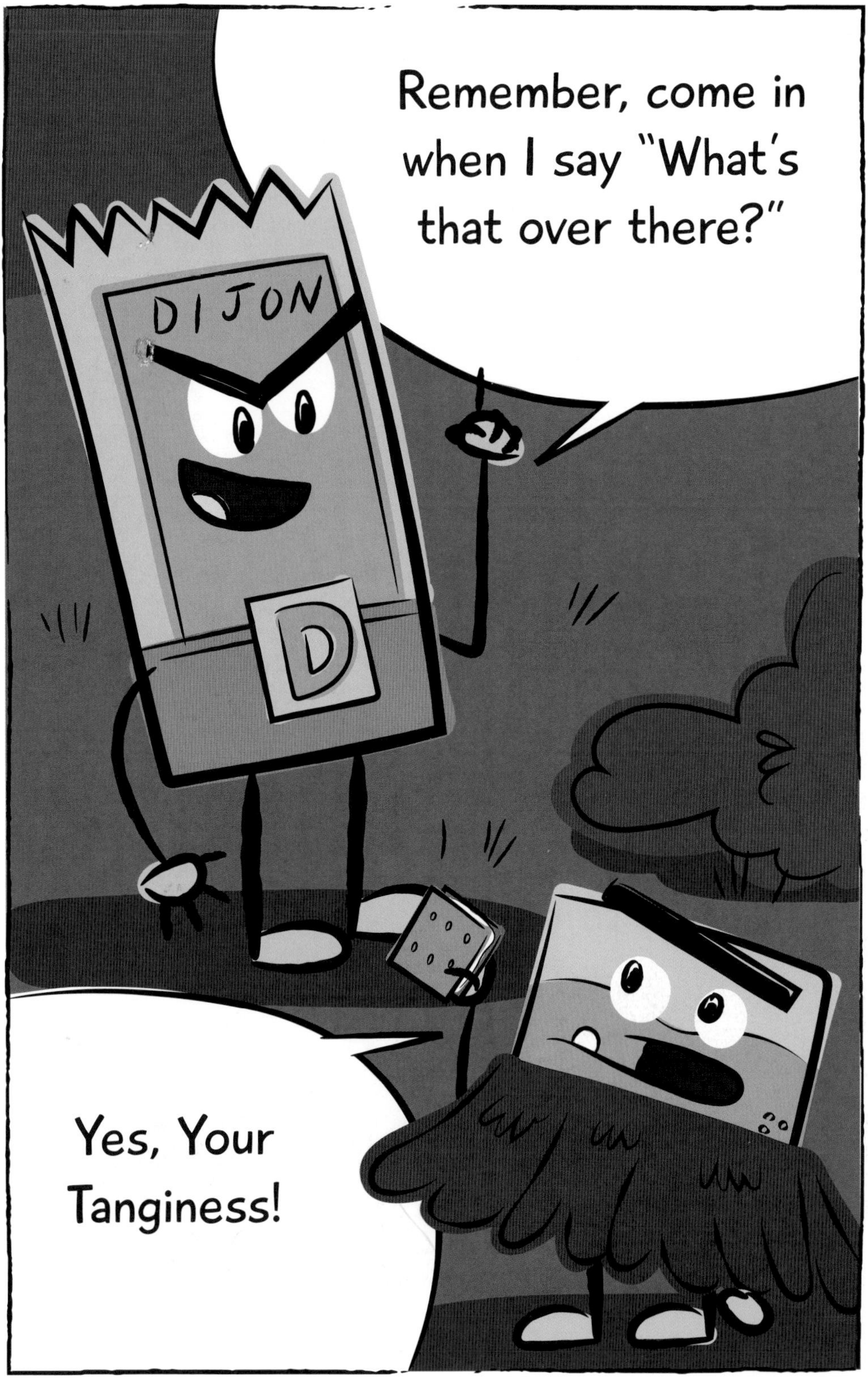
Remember, come in when I say "What's that over there?"
DIJON
D
Yes, Your Tanginess!

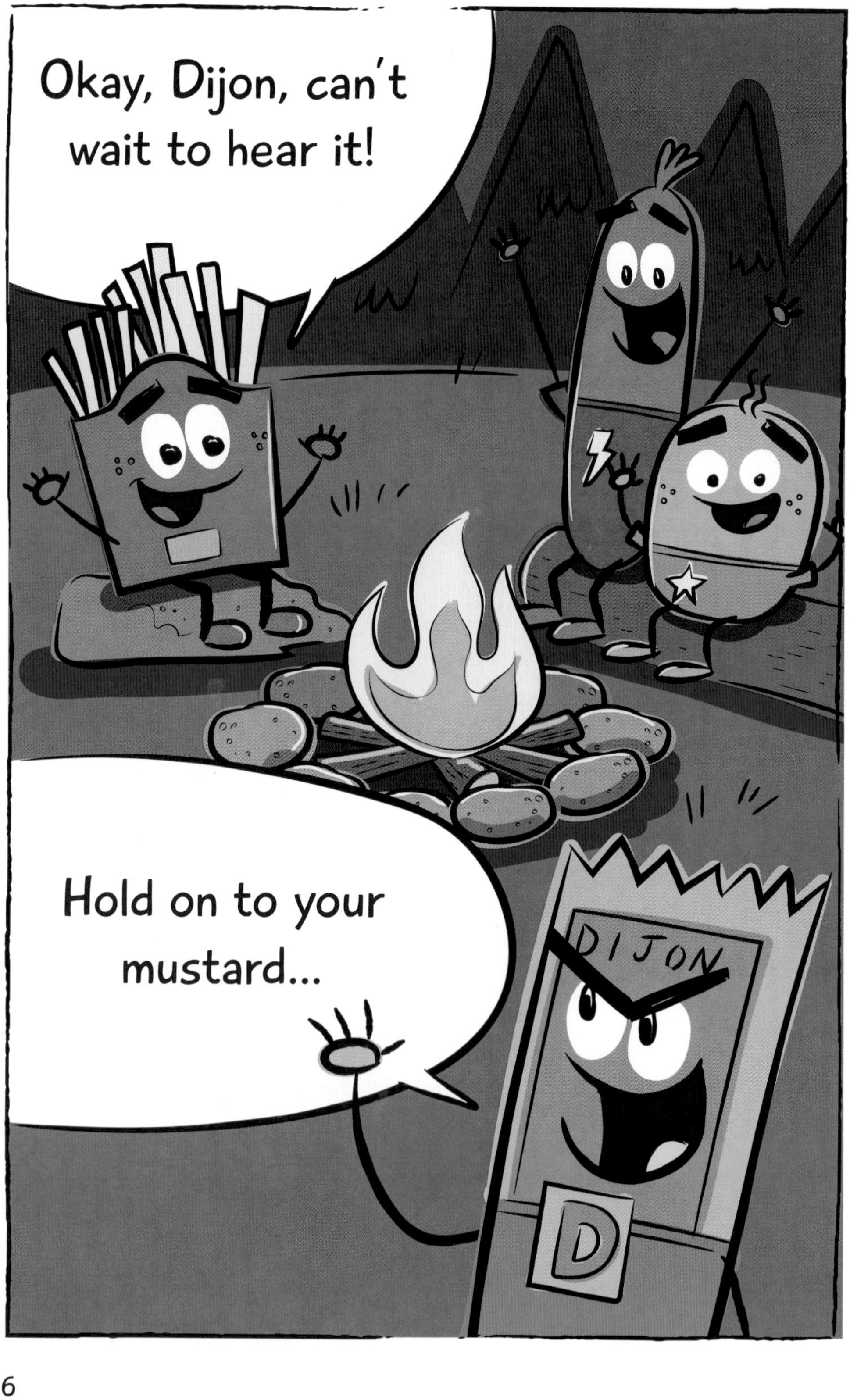
Okay, Dijon, can't wait to hear it!
Hold on to your mustard...
DIJON
D

Chapter 5

THE MEAN GREEN PINE THING

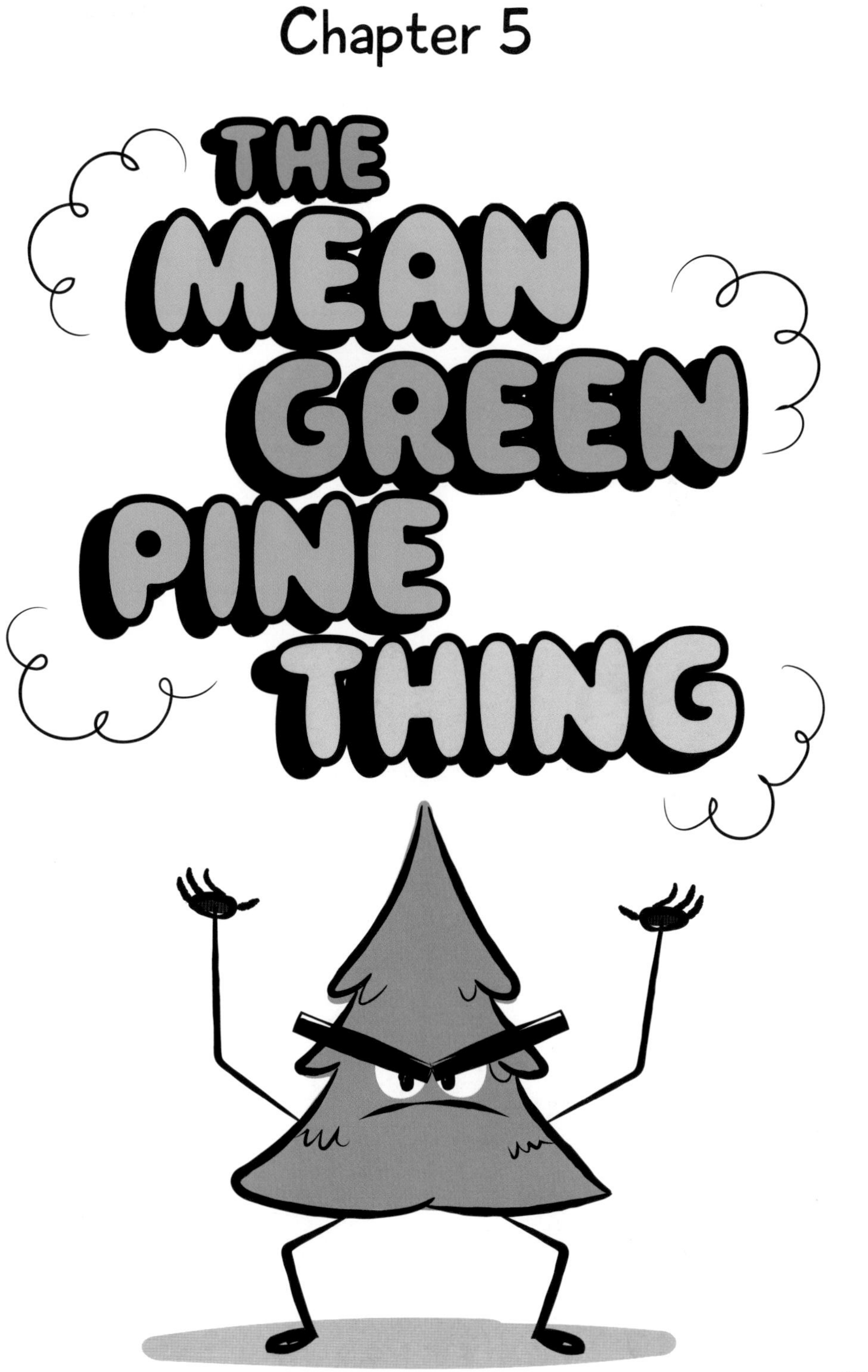

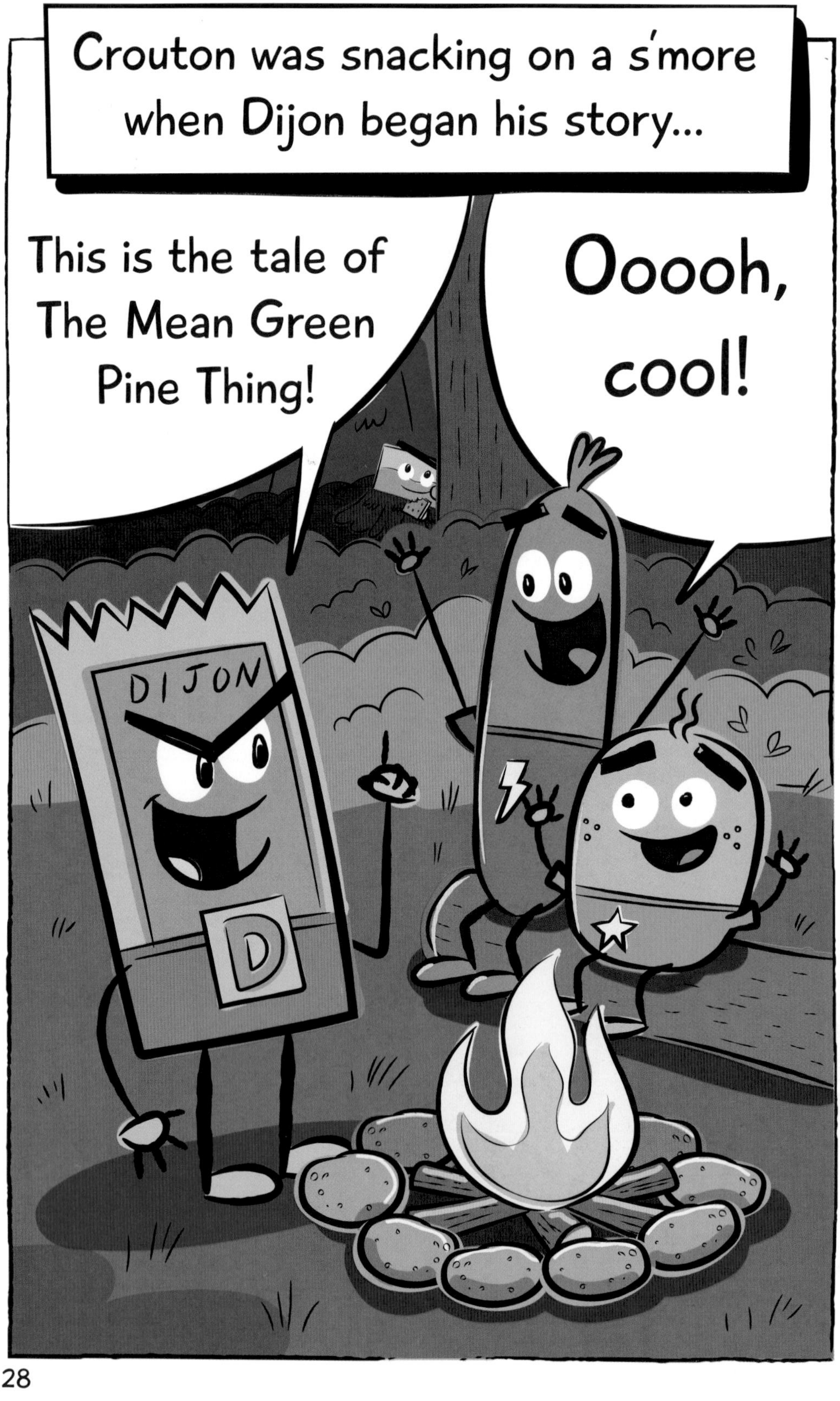
Crouton was snacking on a s'more when Dijon began his story...
This is the tale of The Mean Green Pine Thing!
Ooooh, cool!
DIJON
D

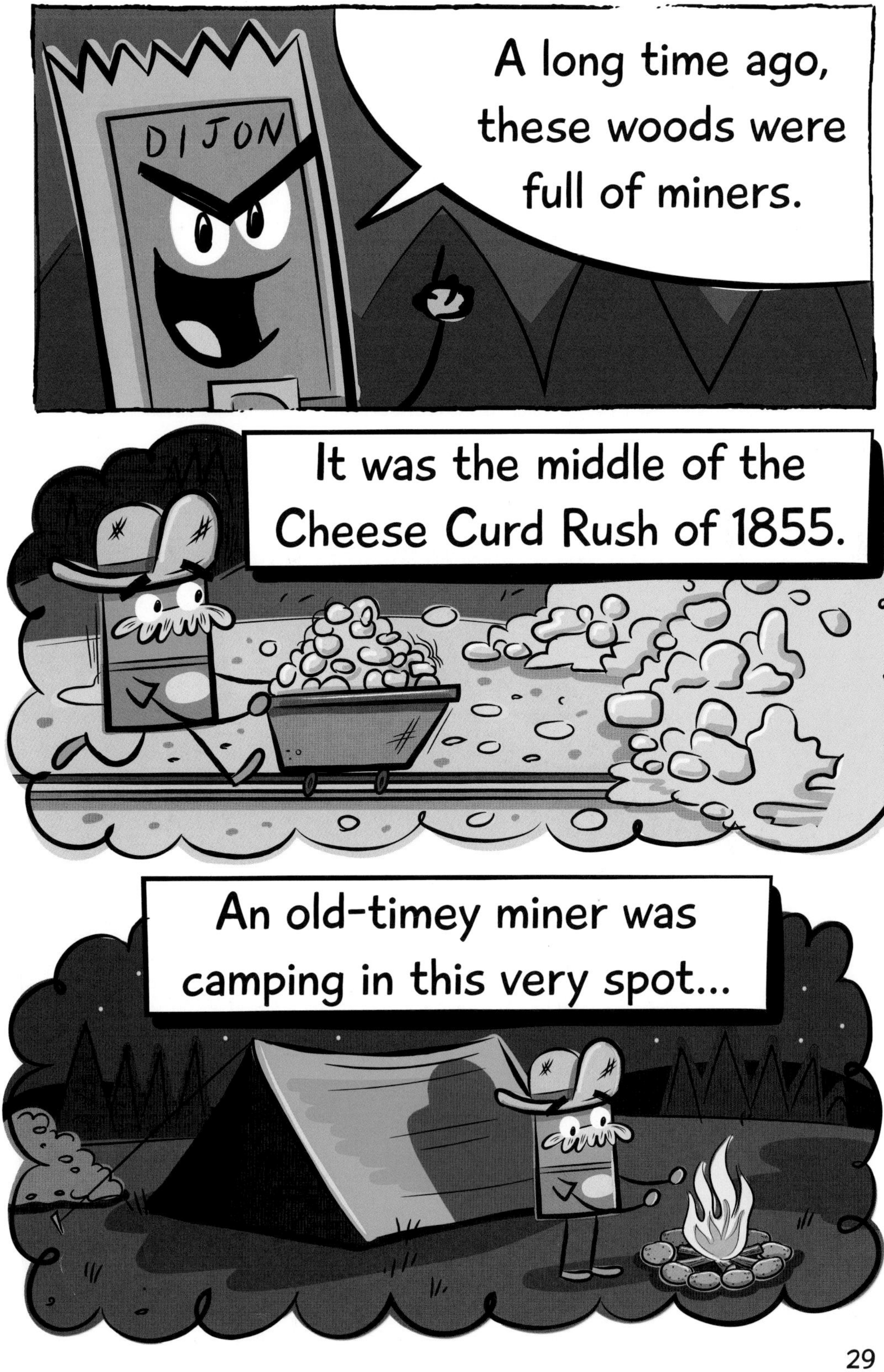
A long time ago, these woods were full of miners.
DIJON
It was the middle of the Cheese Curd Rush of 1855.
An old-timey miner was camping in this very spot...

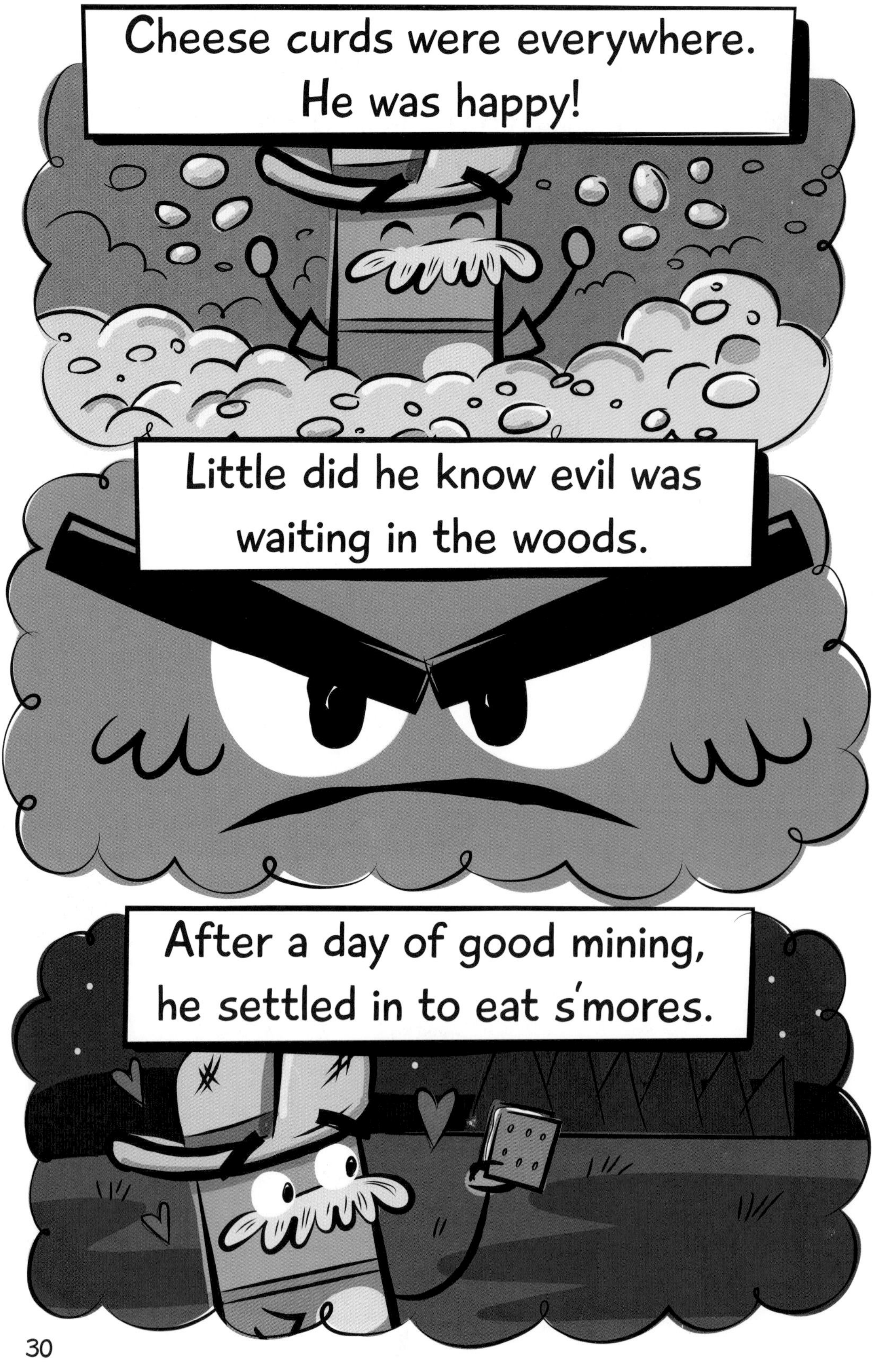
Cheese curds were everywhere. He was happy!
Little did he know evil was waiting in the woods.
After a day of good mining, he settled in to eat s'mores.

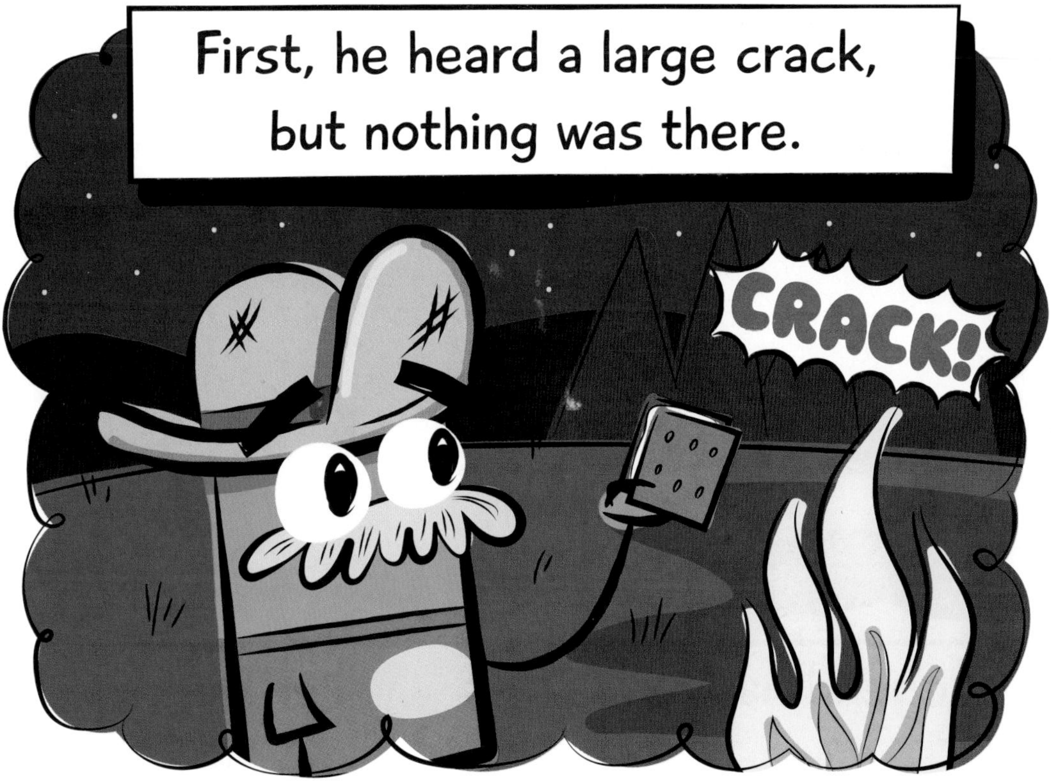
First, he heard a large crack, but nothing was there.
CRACK!

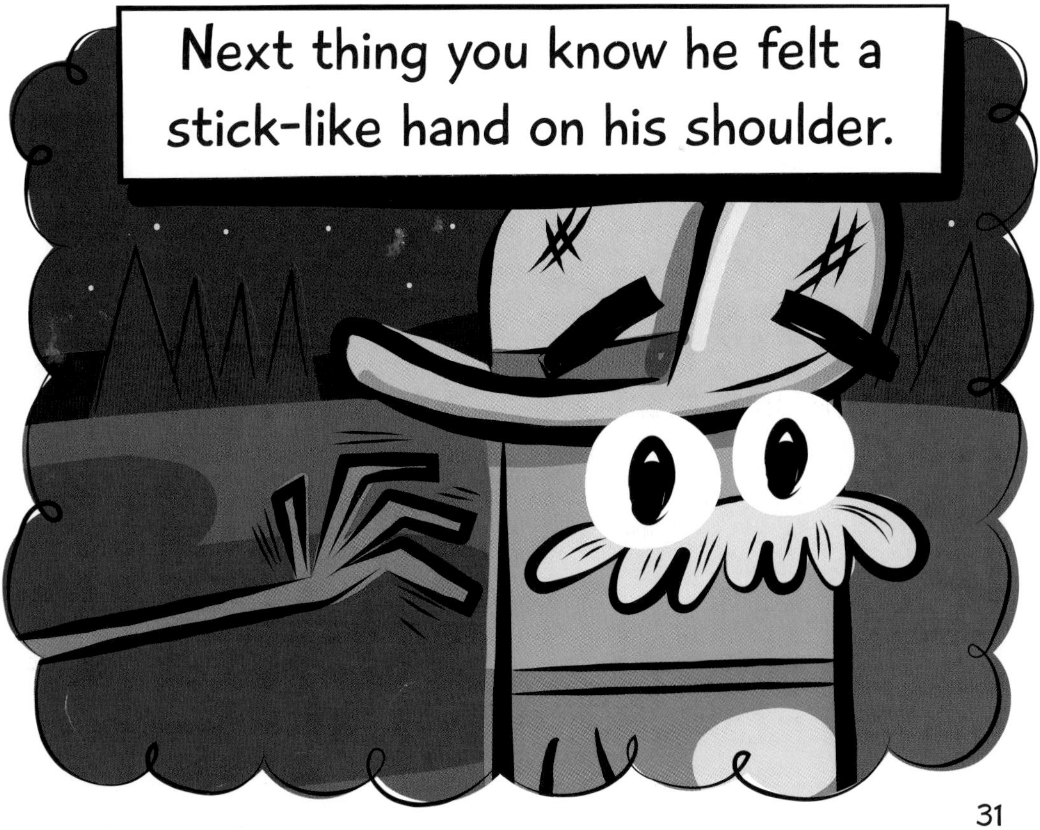
Next thing you know he felt a stick-like hand on his shoulder.

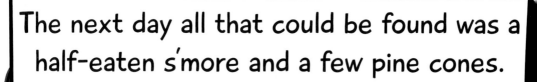

The next day all that could be found was a half-eaten s'more and a few pine cones.

Legend has it, he was whisked away by The Mean Green Pine Thing. And The Mean Green Pine Thing is still out there.

Whoa, that was scary!

What's that over there?!

Chapter 6

SOMETHING'S STICKY

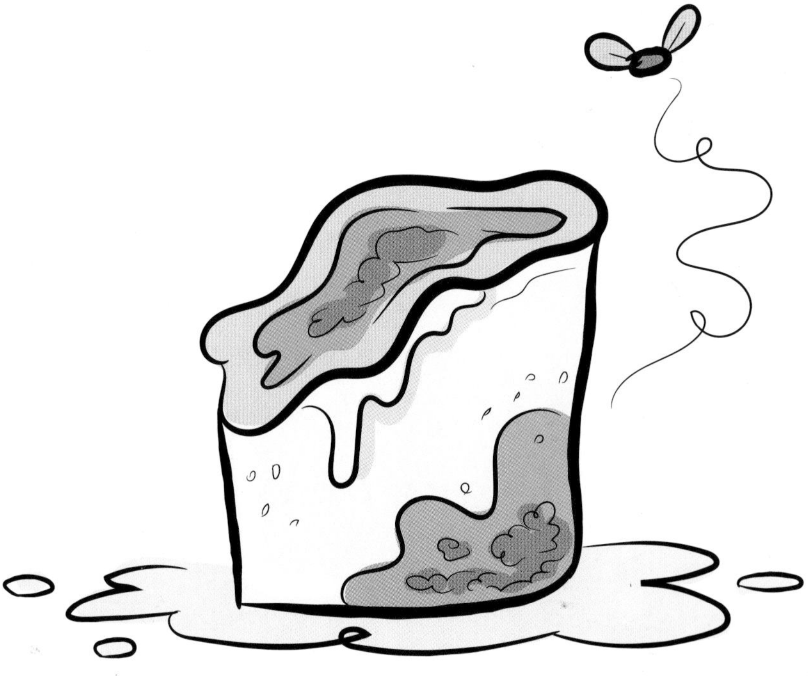

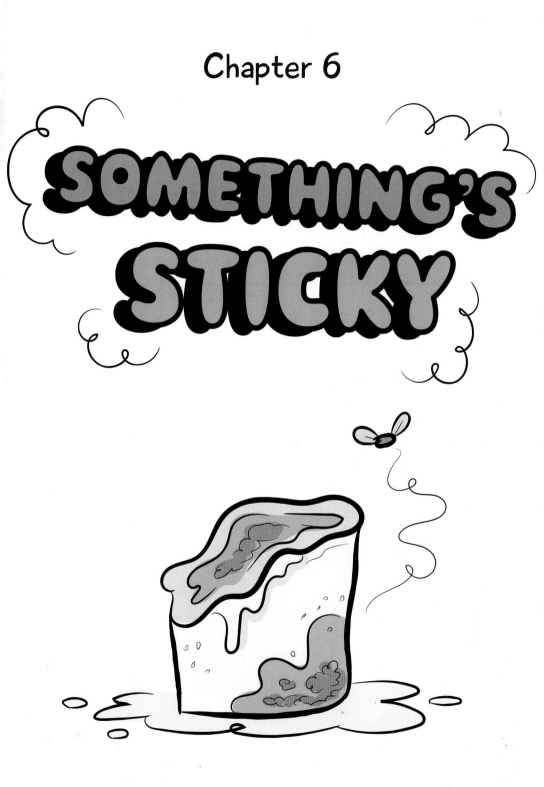

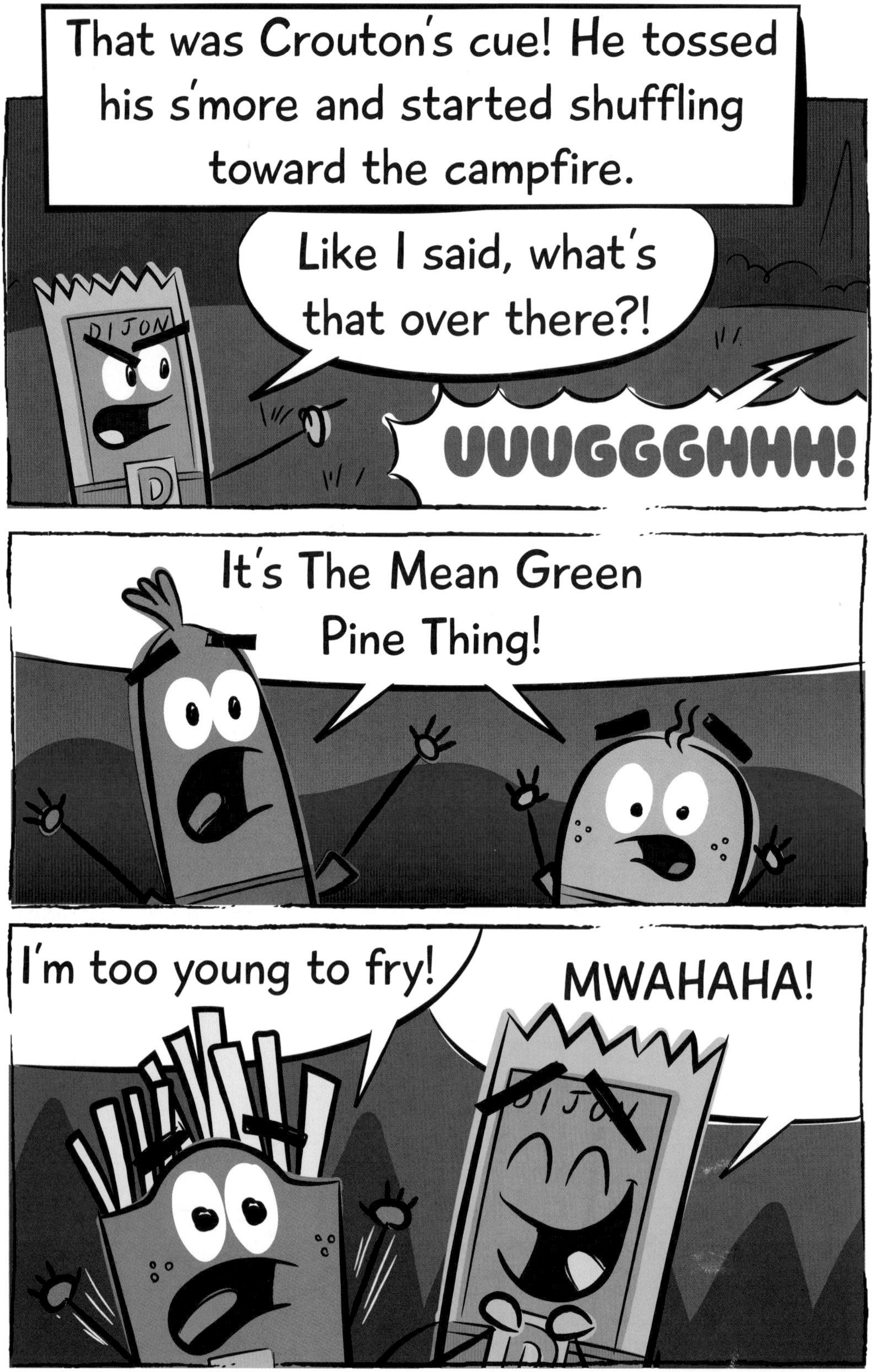
That was Crouton's cue! He tossed his s'more and started shuffling toward the campfire.
Like I said, what's that over there?!
DIJON
UUUGGGHHH!
It's The Mean Green Pine Thing!
I'm too young to fry!
MWAHAHA!

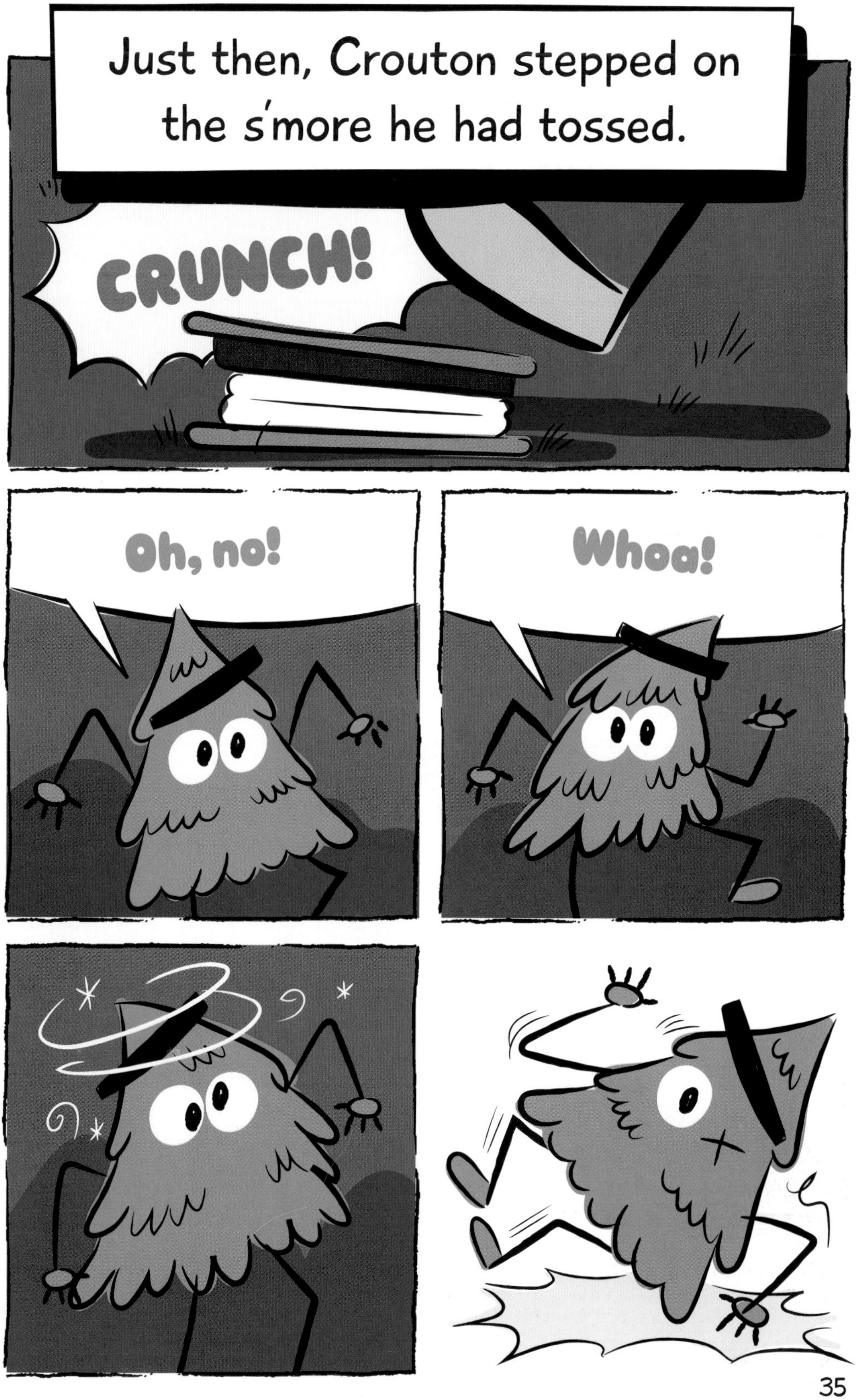
Just then, Crouton stepped on the s'more he had tossed.
CRUNCH!
Oh, no!
Whoa!

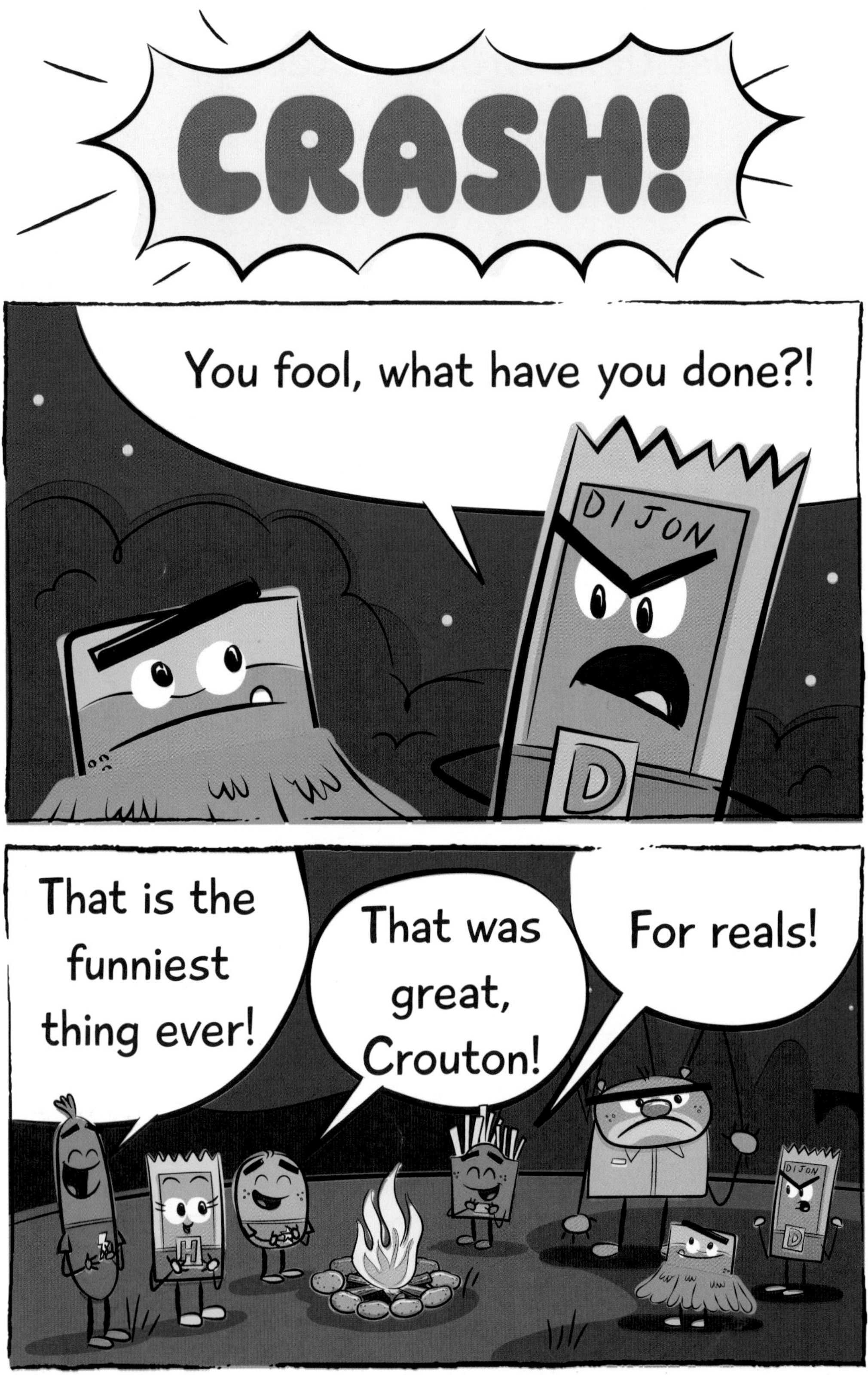
CRASH!
You fool, what have you done?!
DIJON
D
That is the funniest thing ever!
That was great, Crouton!
For reals!

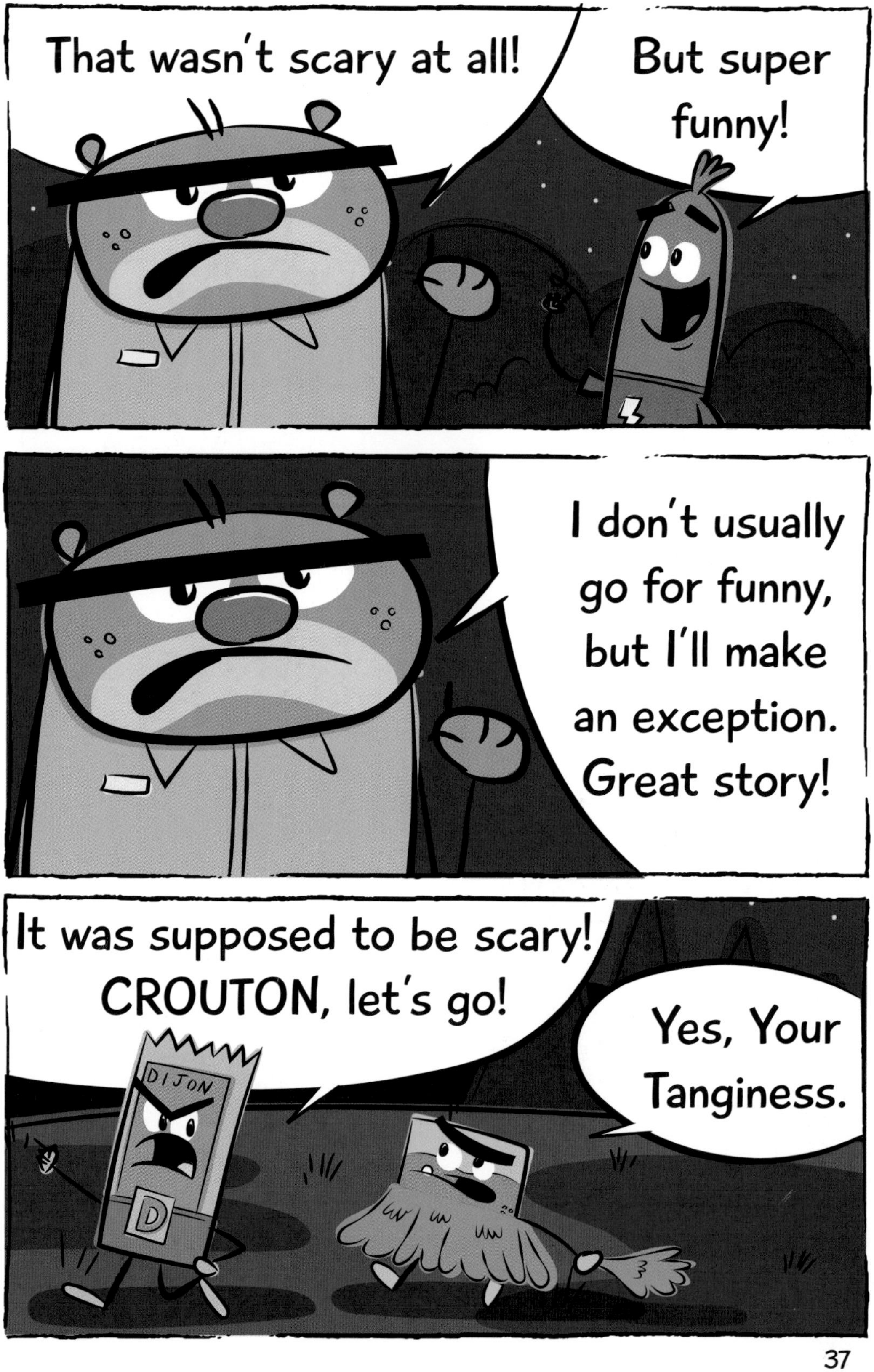
That wasn't scary at all!
But super funny!
I don't usually go for funny, but I'll make an exception. Great story!
It was supposed to be scary! CROUTON, let's go!
Yes, Your Tanginess.
DIJON
D

Chapter 7

LAUGH IT UP!

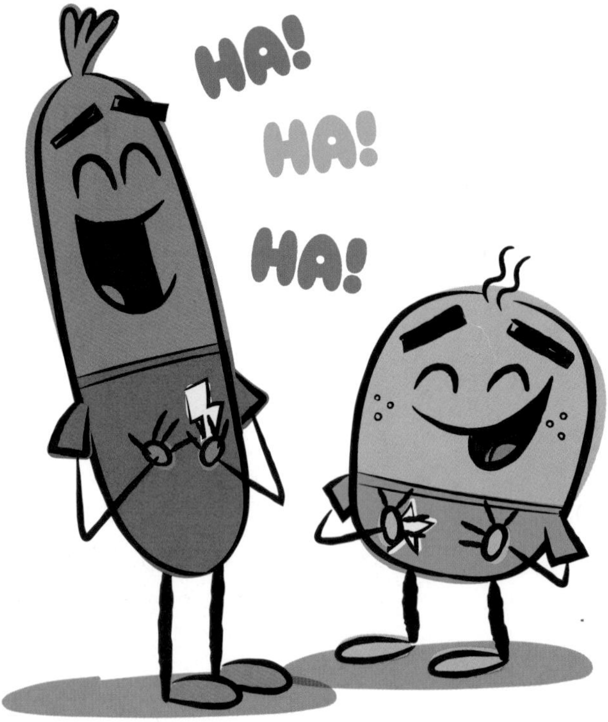
HA!
HA!
HA!

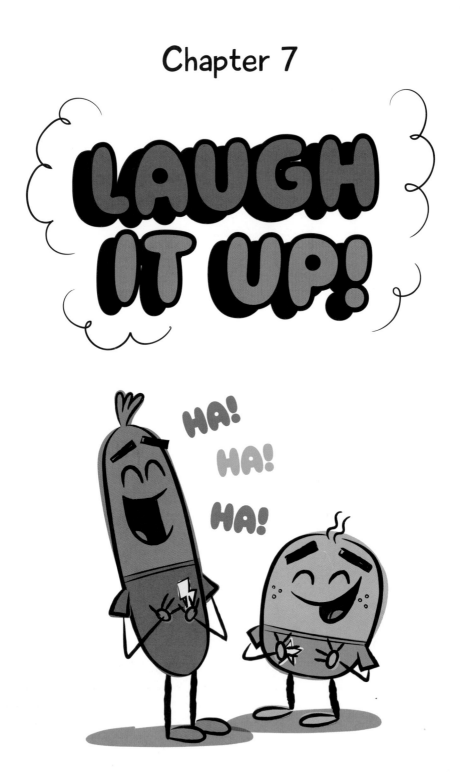

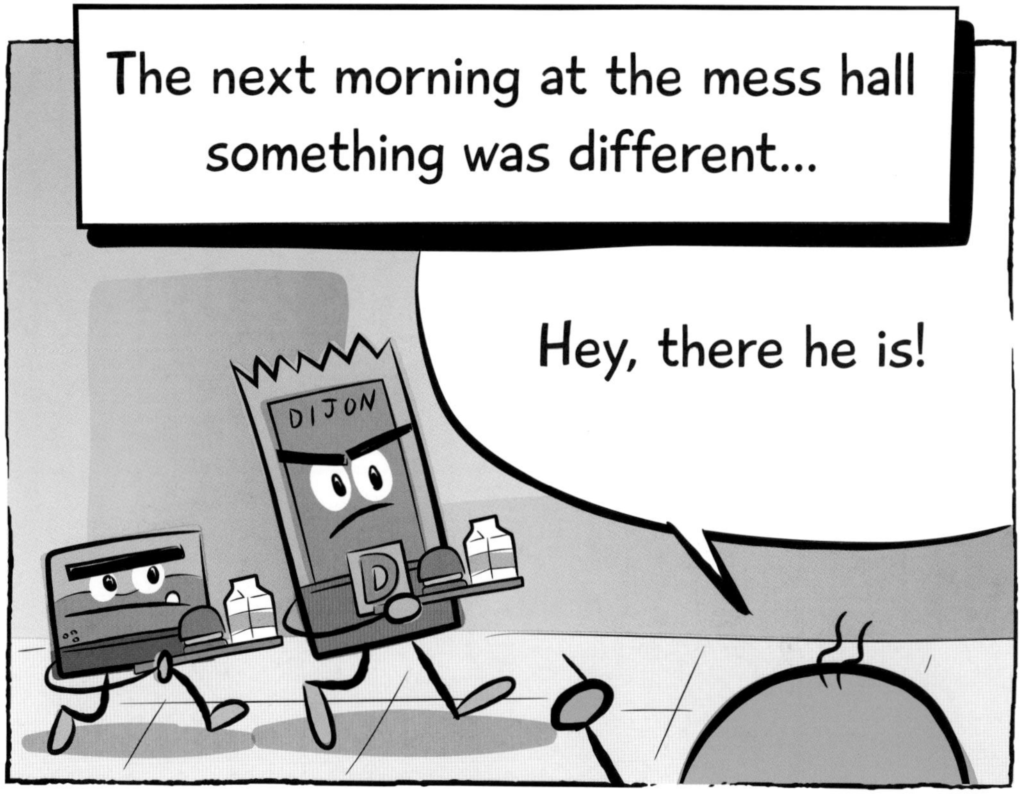
The next morning at the mess hall something was different...
Hey, there he is!
DIJON
D

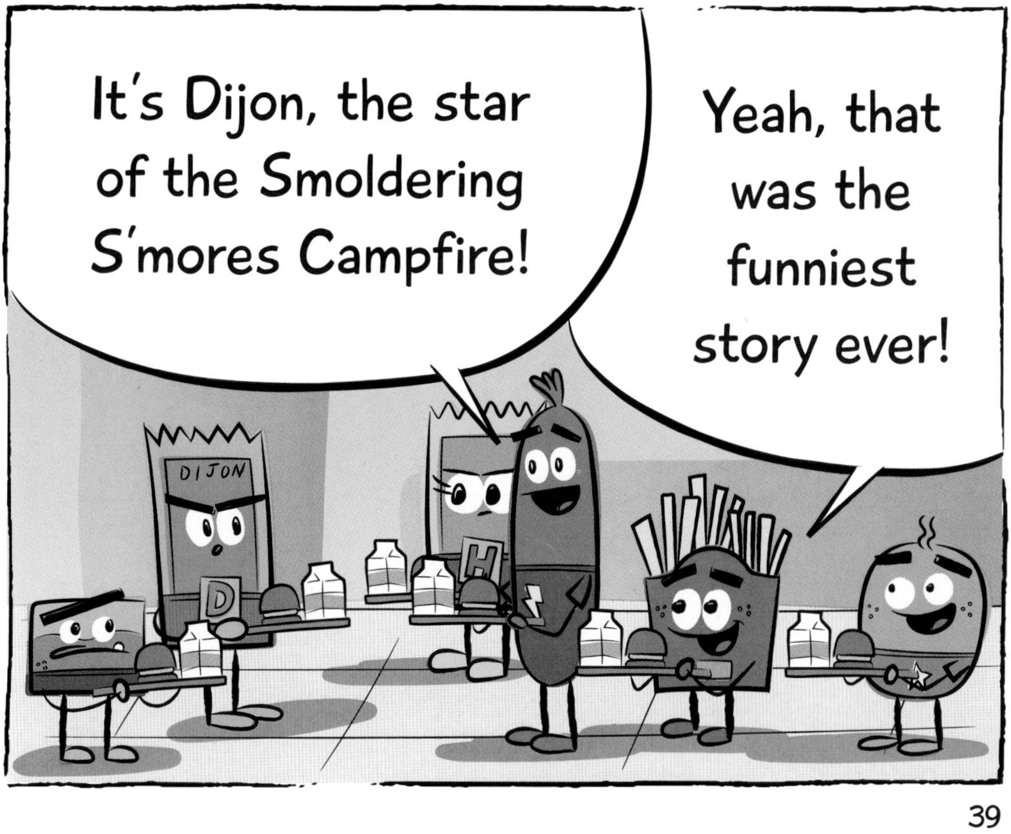
It's Dijon, the star of the Smoldering S'mores Campfire!
Yeah, that was the funniest story ever!
DIJON
D
H

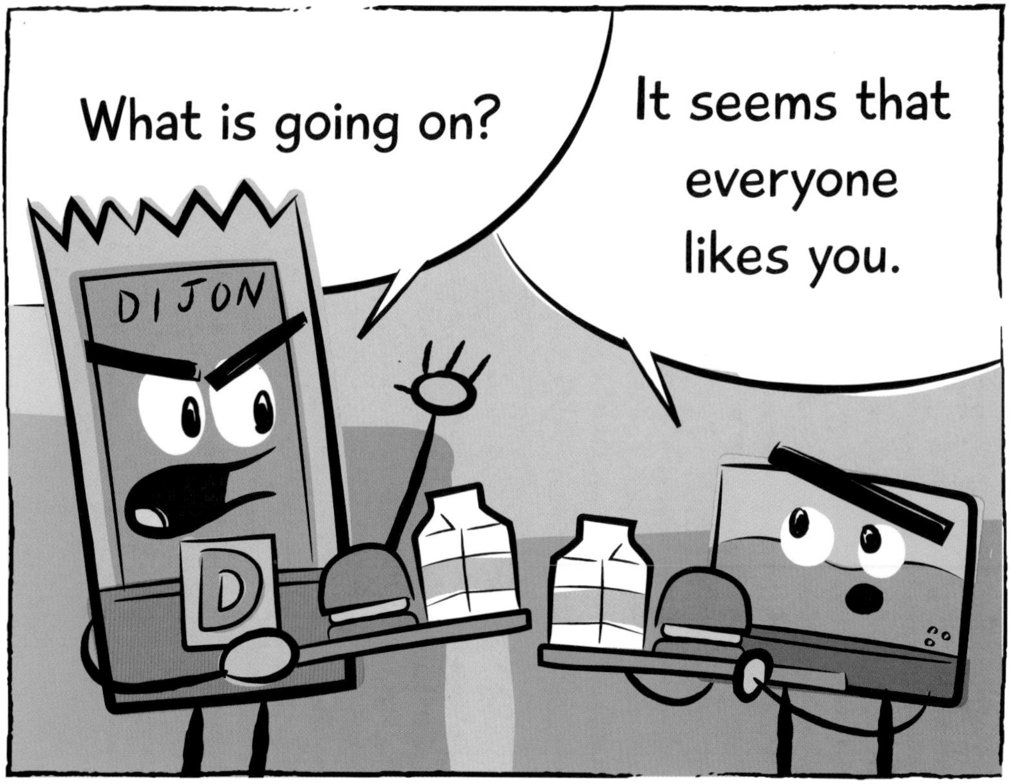
What is going on?
It seems that everyone likes you.
DIJON
D

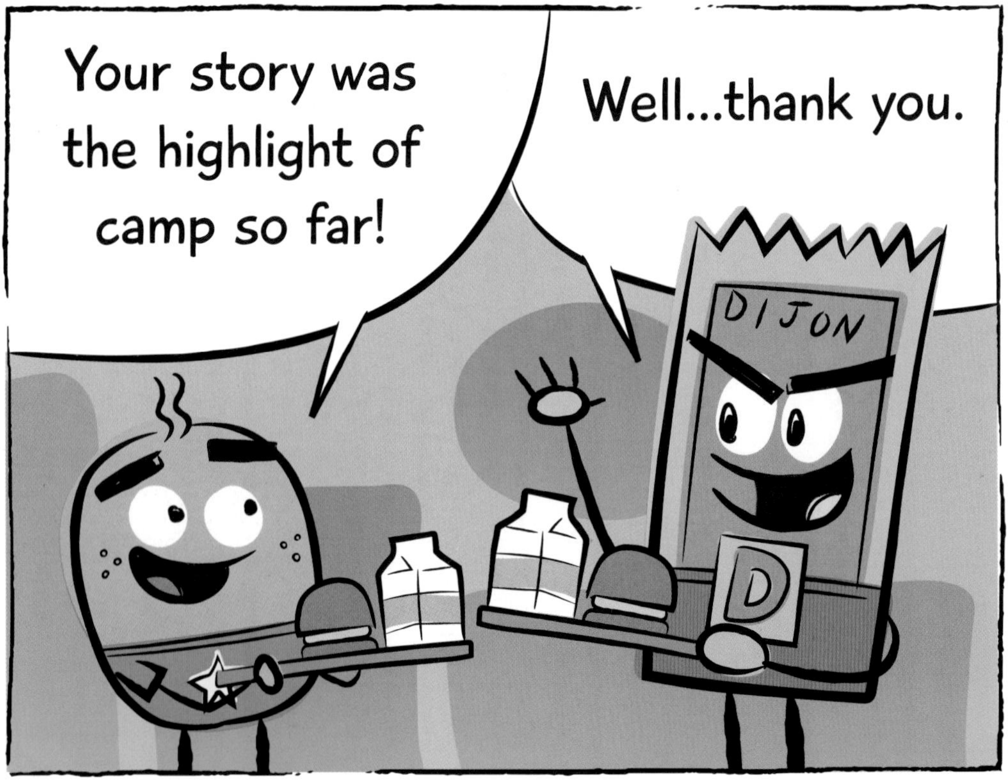
Your story was the highlight of camp so far!
Well...thank you.
DIJON
D

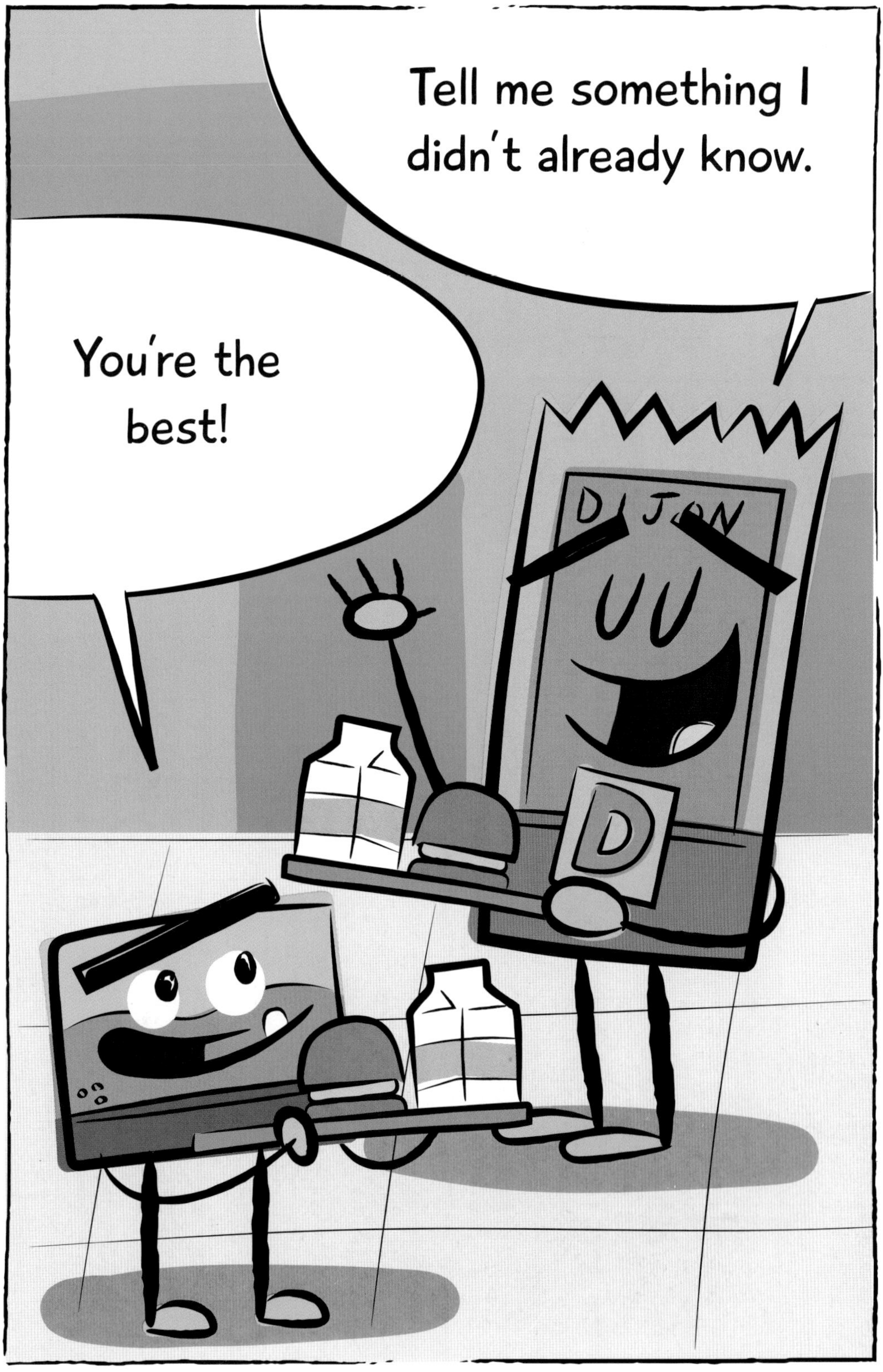
You're the best!
Tell me something I didn't already know.
DIJON
D

Chapter 8

TAKE A HIKE

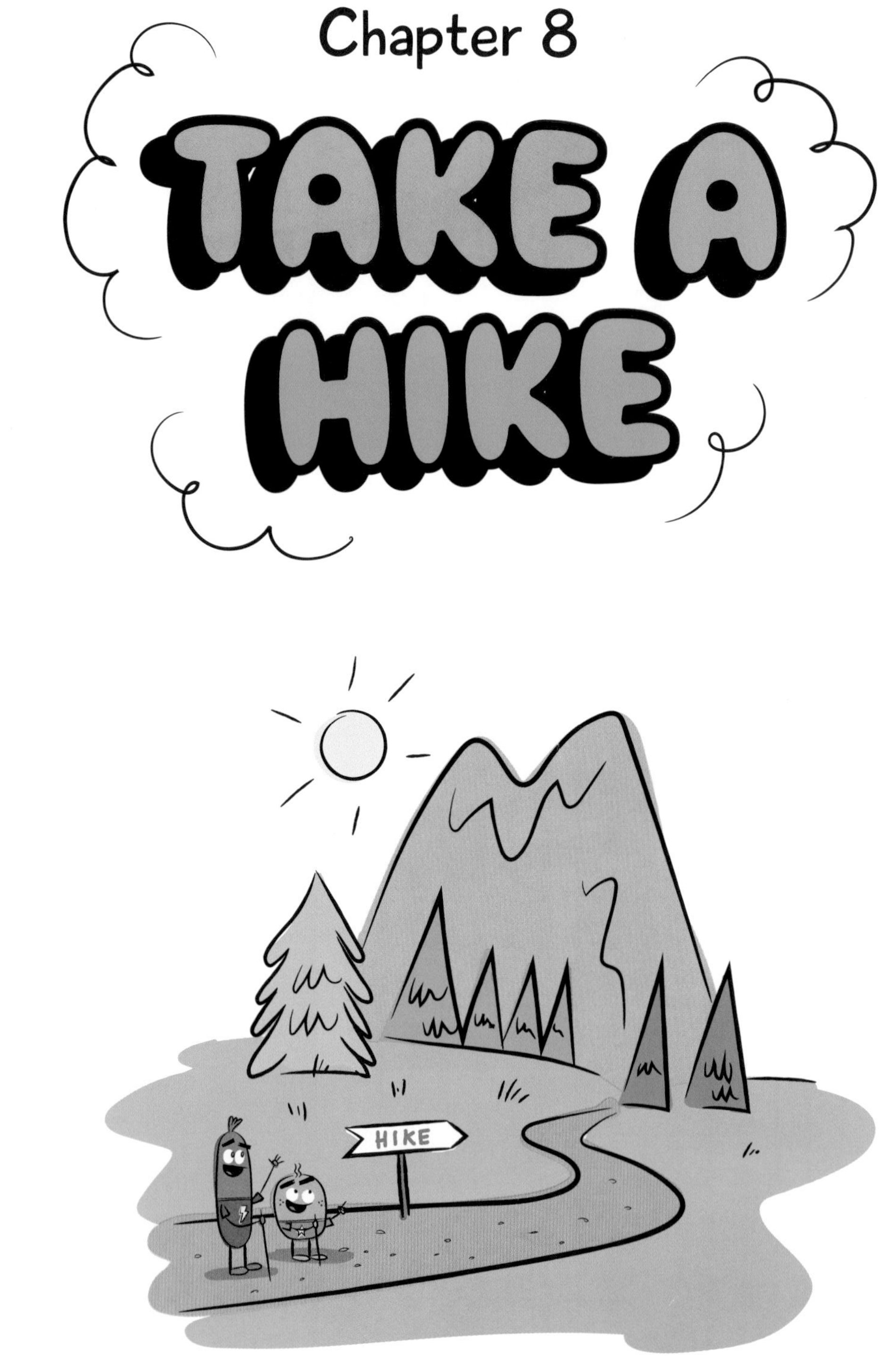
HIKE

Dijon was still enjoying his fame later as the campers started out on their night hike.

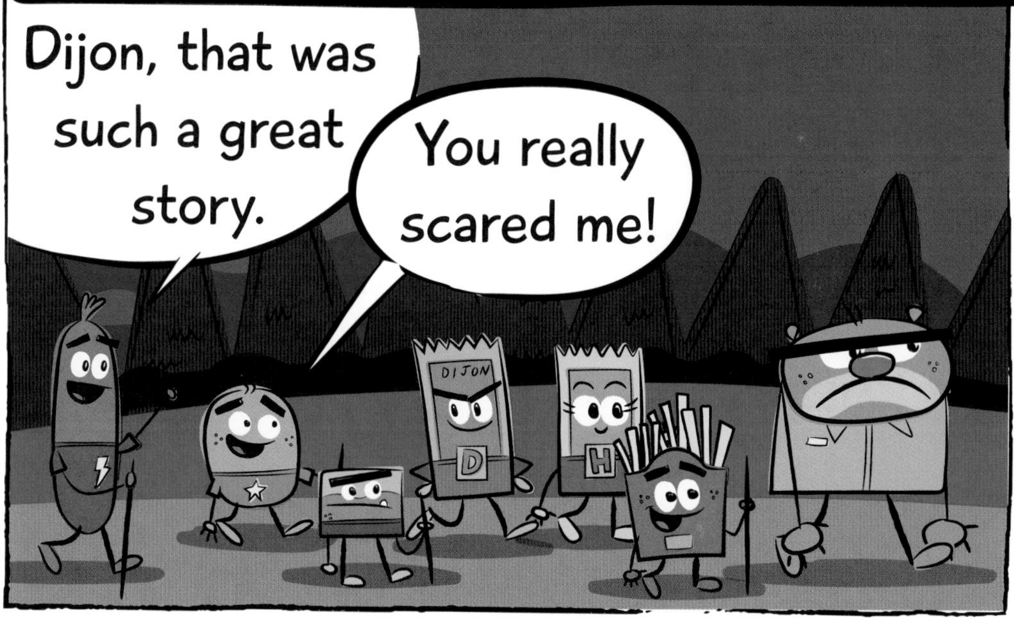
Dijon, that was such a great story.
You really scared me!
DIJON

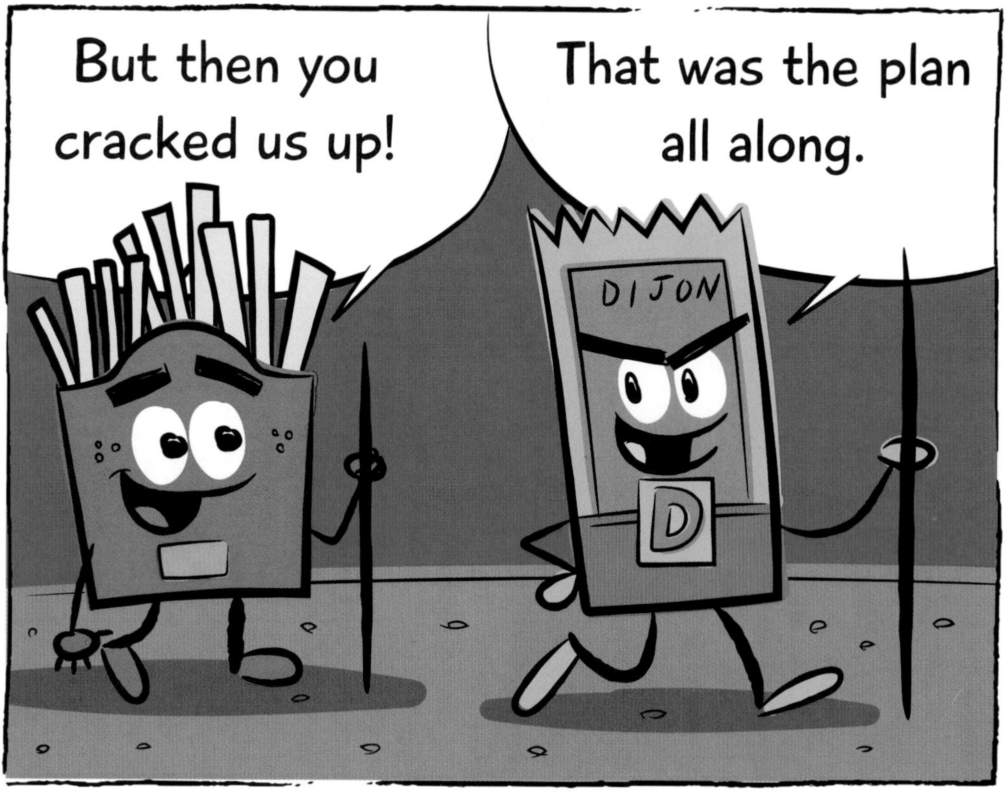
But then you cracked us up!
That was the plan all along.
DIJON

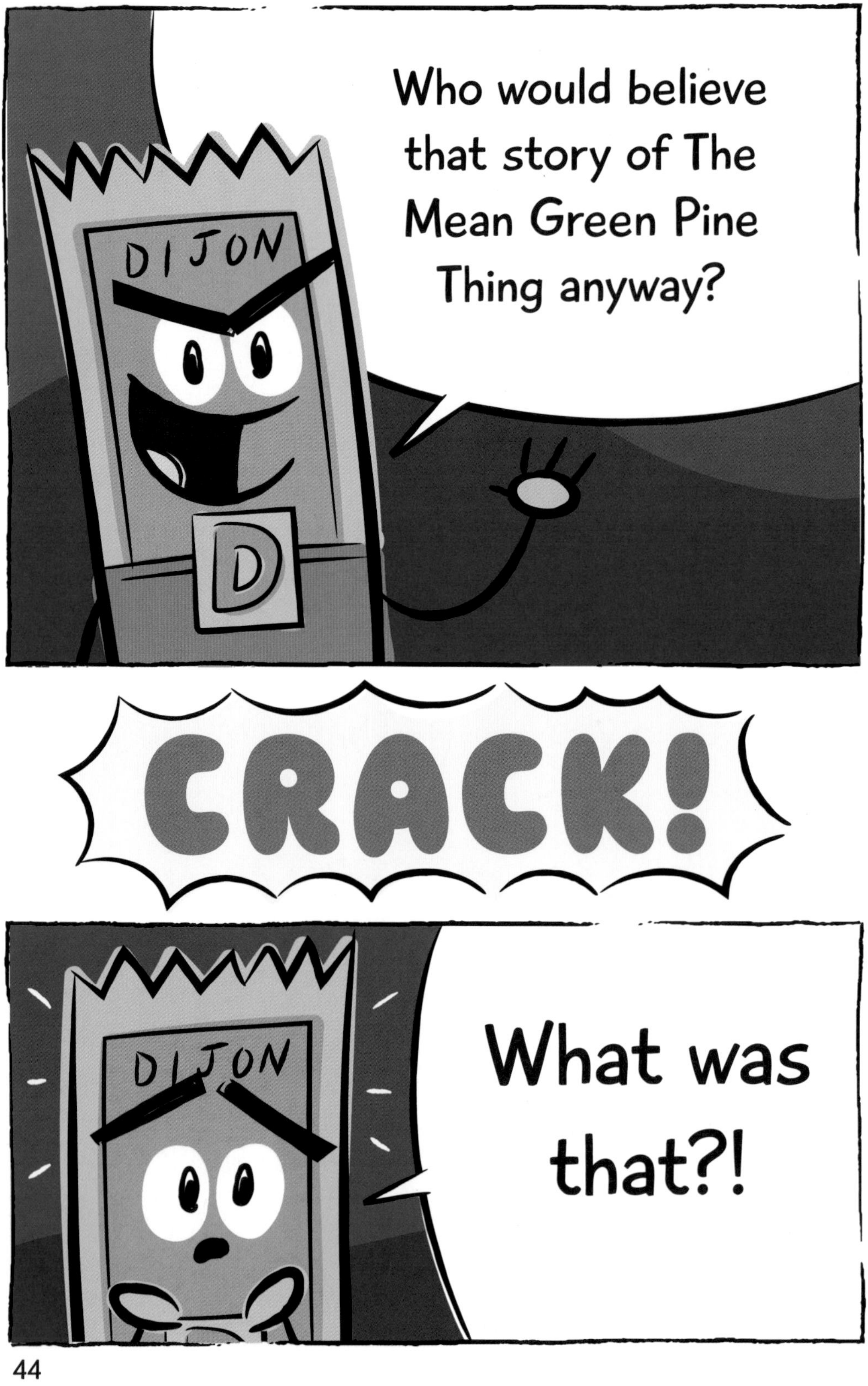
Who would believe that story of The Mean Green Pine Thing anyway?
DIJON
D
CRACK!
DIJON
What was that?!

Just then, the campers found themselves face to face with The Mean Green Pine Thing.
Relax, everyone, it's just Crouton.
DIJON

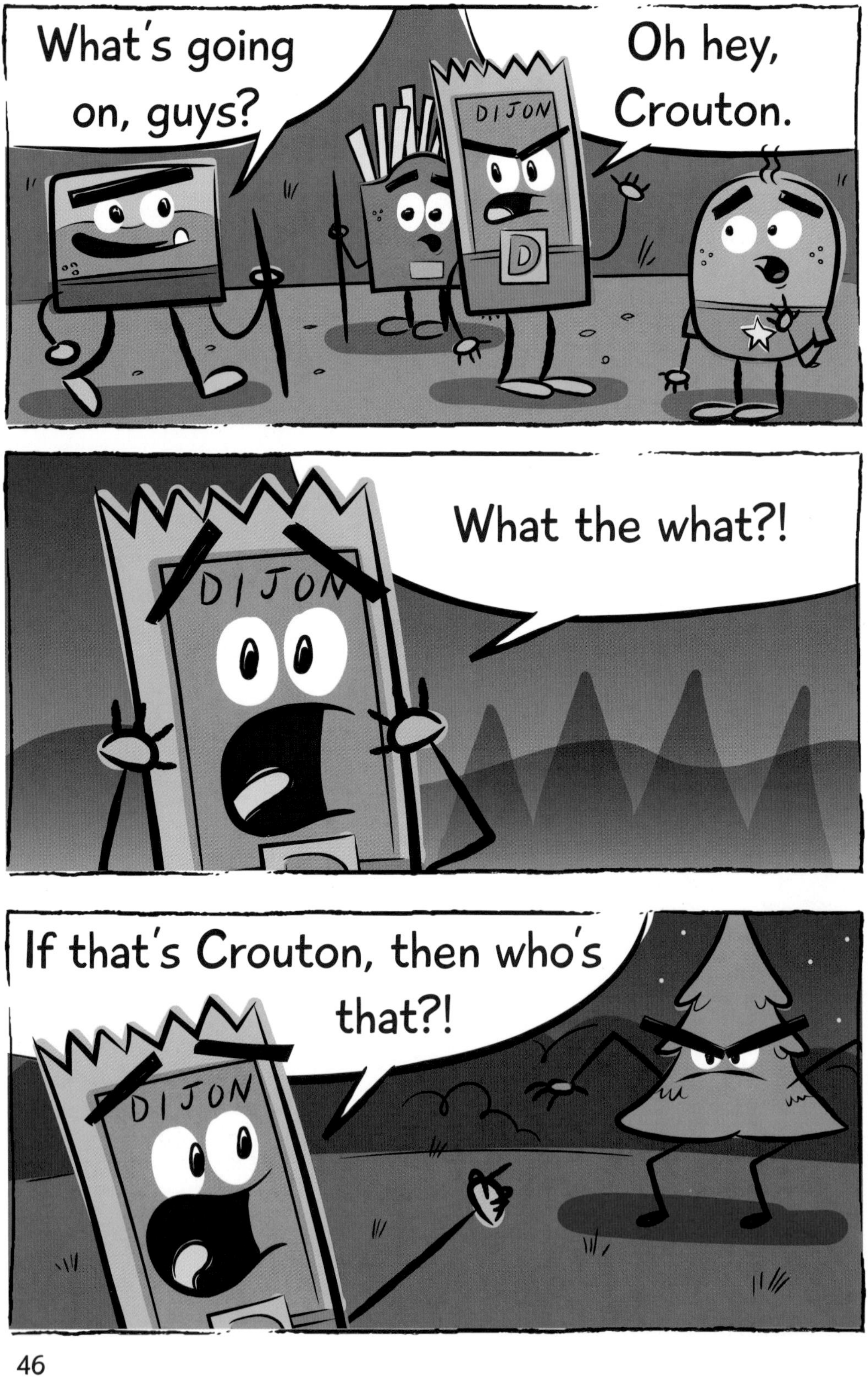
What's going on, guys?
Oh hey, Crouton.
DIJON
D
What the what?!
DIJON
If that's Crouton, then who's that?!
DIJON

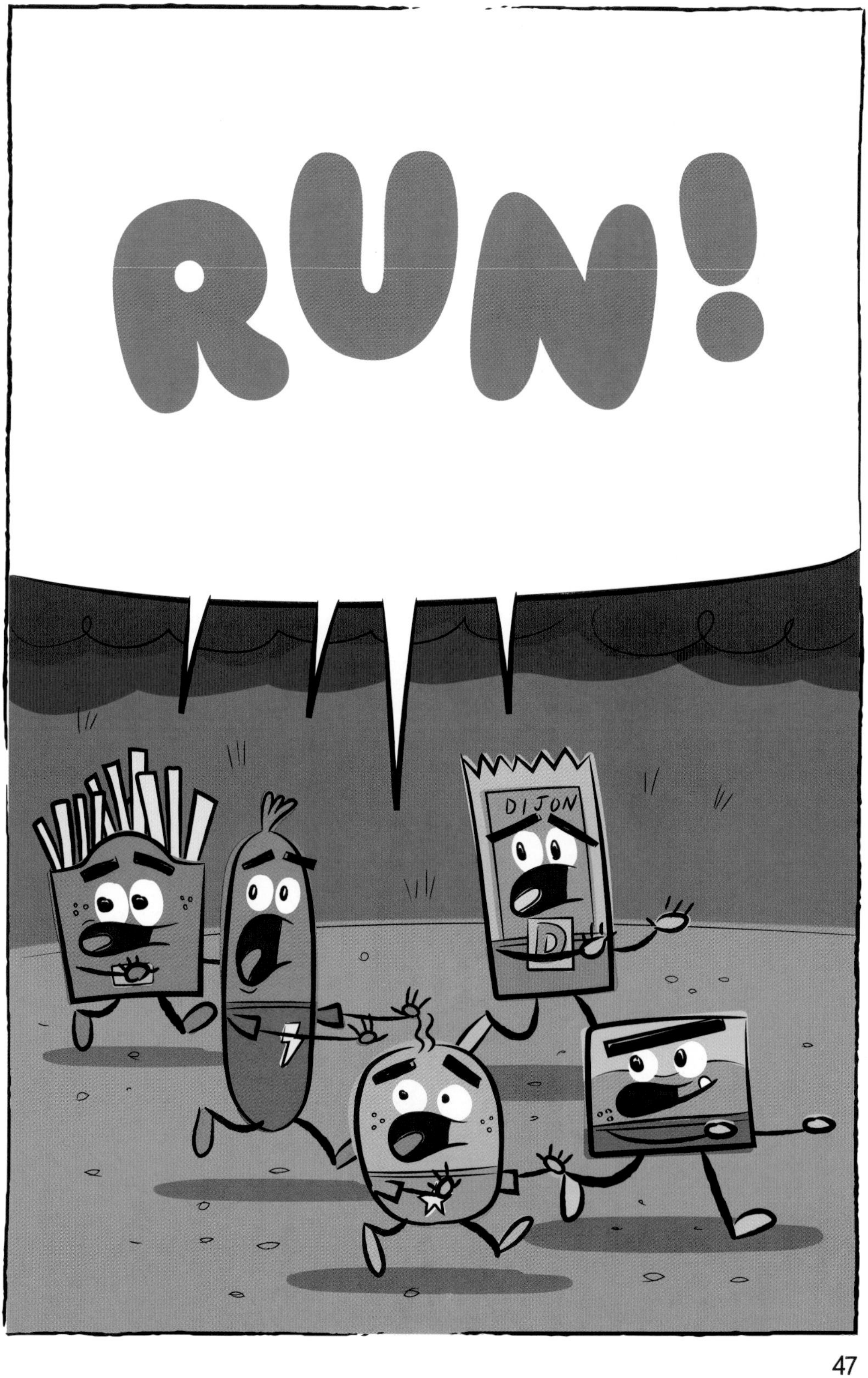
RUN!
DIJON
D

Chapter 9

BRAVE AND SPICY

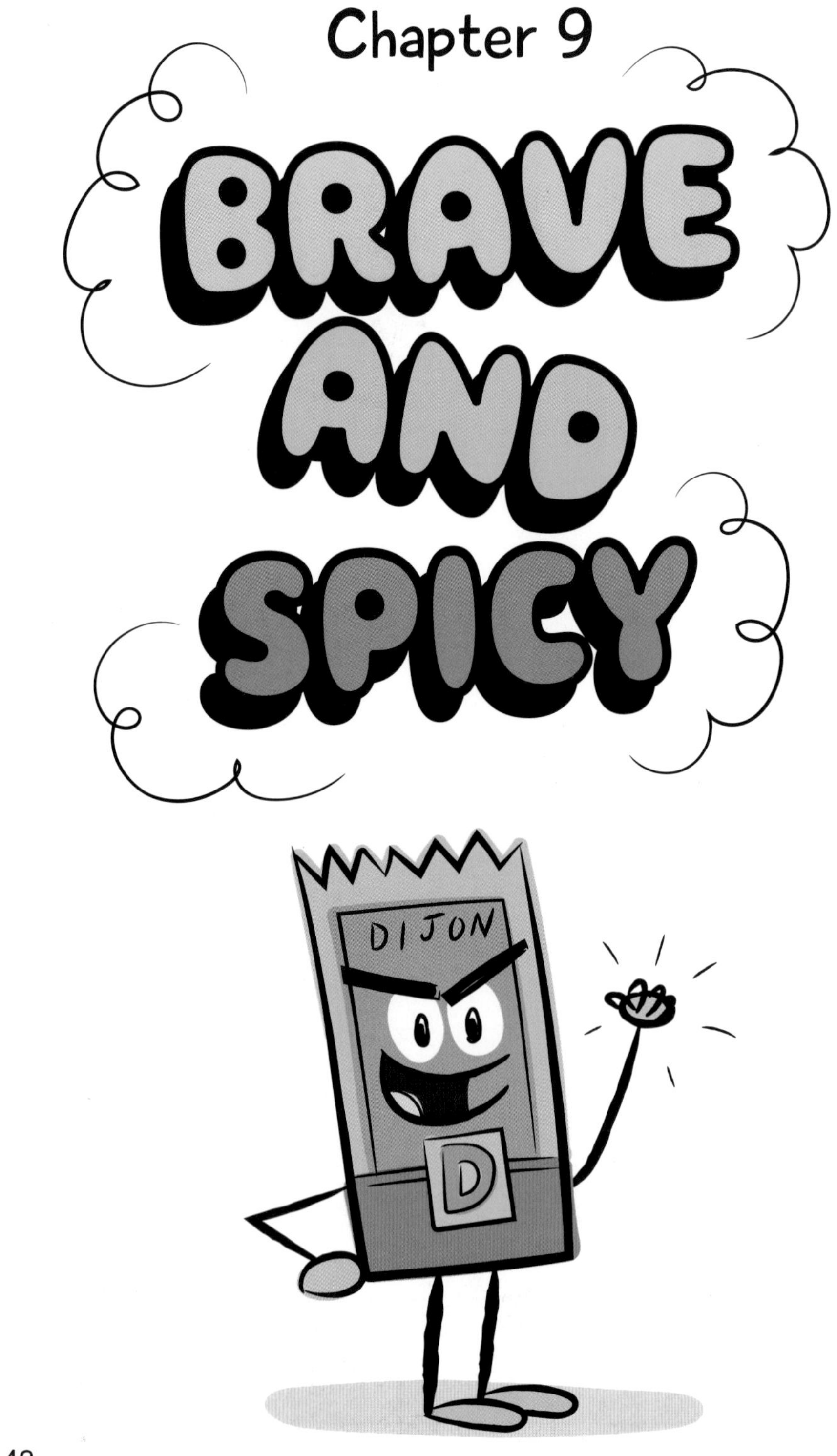
DIJON
D

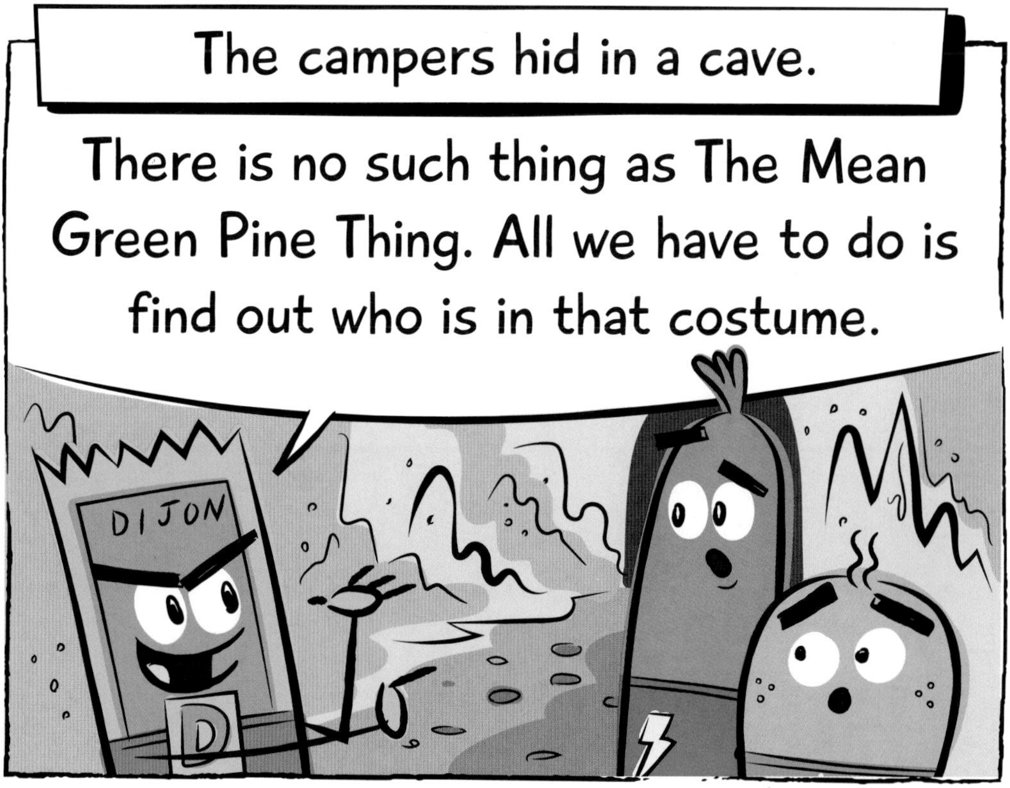
The campers hid in a cave.
There is no such thing as The Mean Green Pine Thing. All we have to do is find out who is in that costume.
DIJON
D

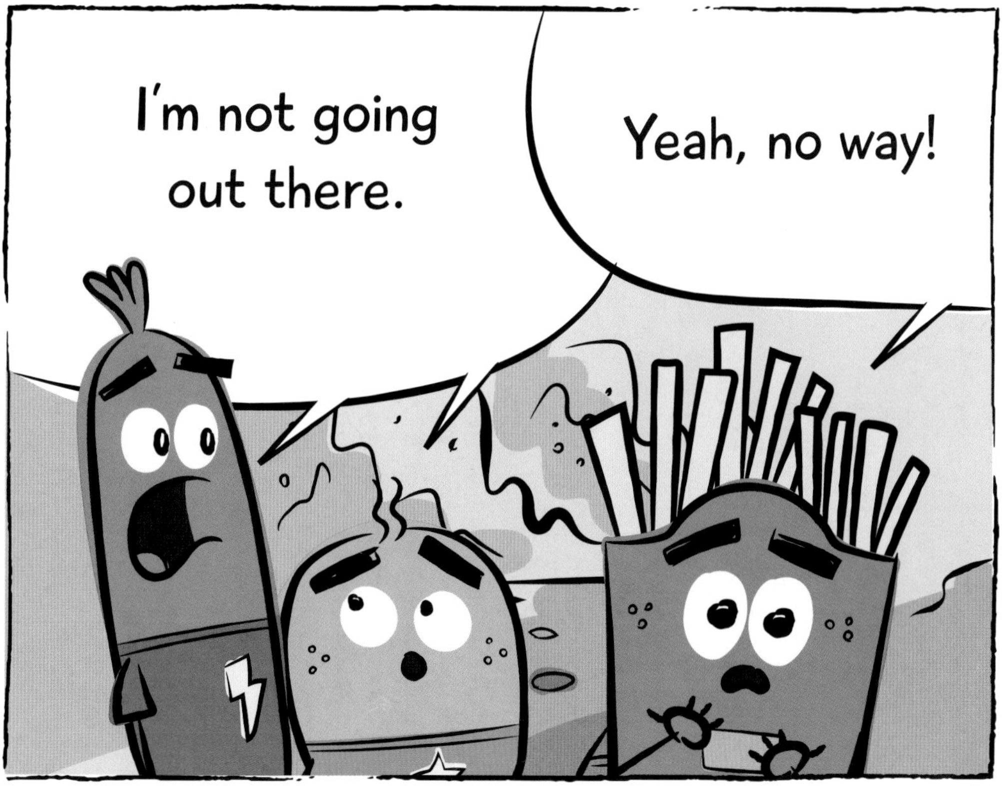
I'm not going out there.
Yeah, no way!

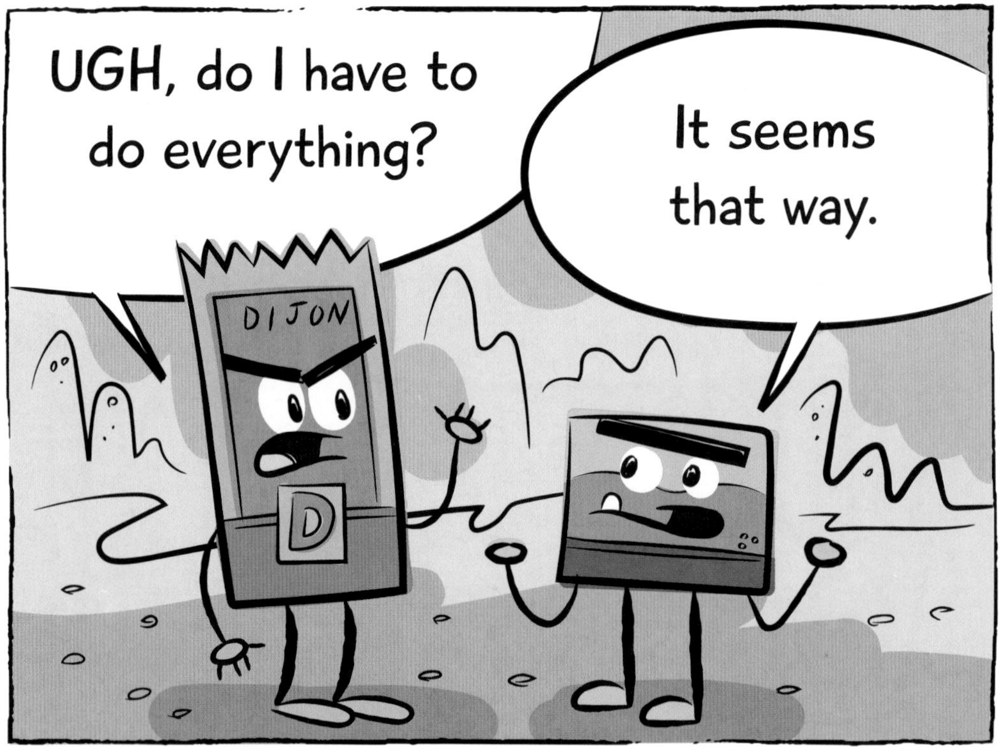
UGH, do I have to do everything?
It seems that way.

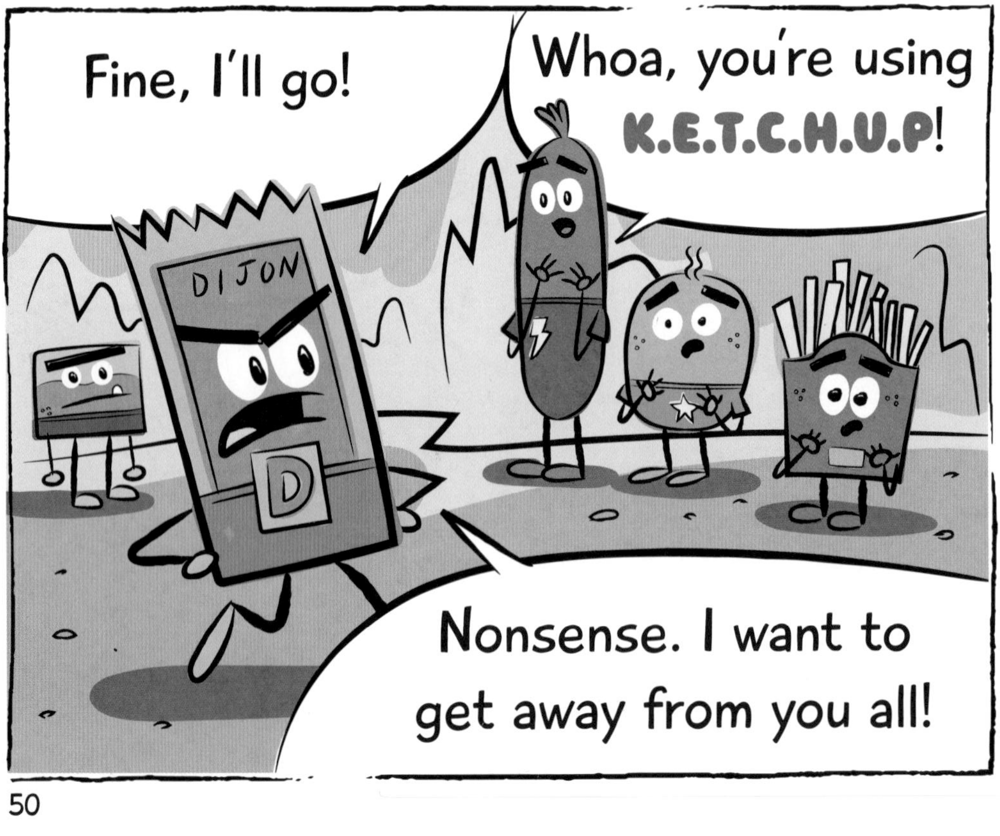
Fine, I'll go!
Whoa, you're using K.E.T.C.H.U.P!
Nonsense. I want to get away from you all!

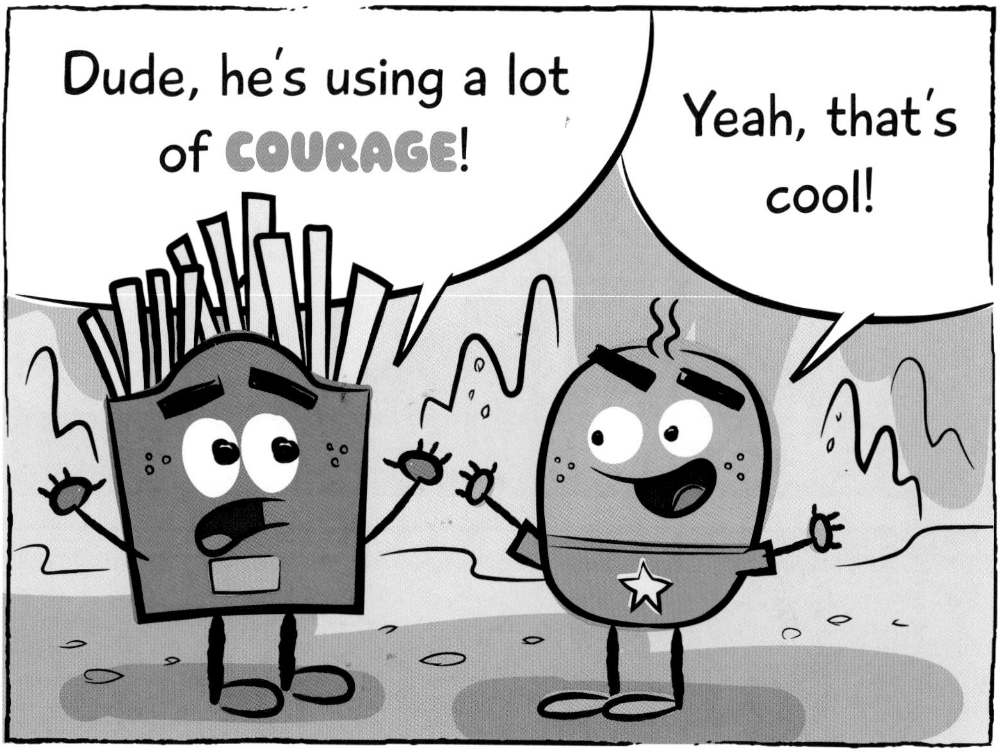
Dude, he's using a lot of COURAGE!
Yeah, that's cool!

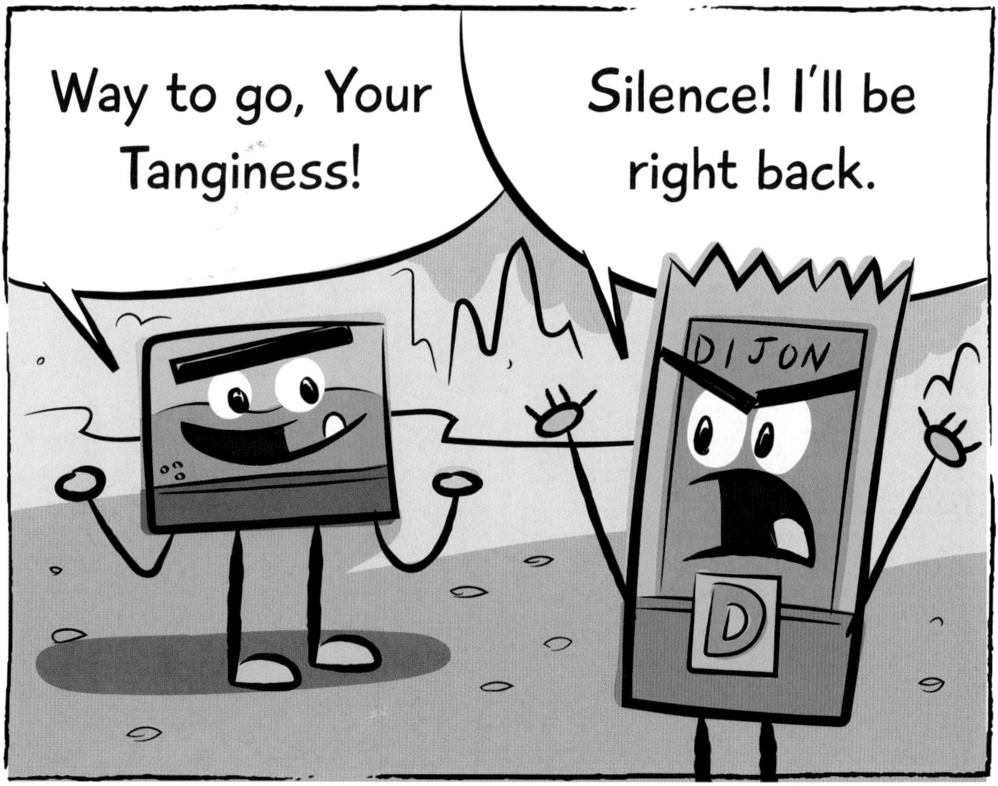
Way to go, Your Tanginess!
Silence! I'll be right back.
DIJON
D

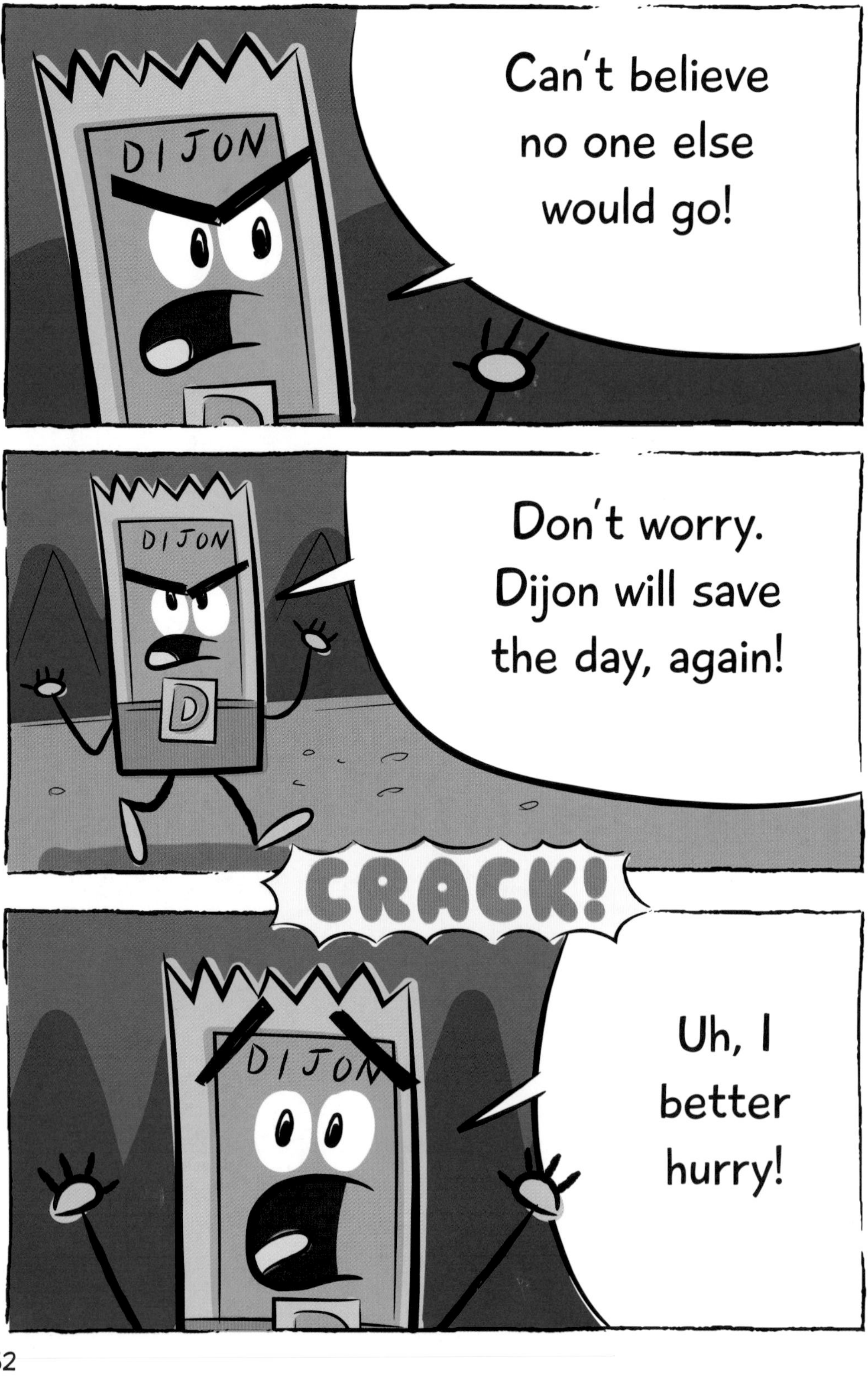
Can't believe no one else would go!
DIJON
Don't worry. Dijon will save the day, again!
DIJON
D
CRACK!
DIJON
Uh, I better hurry!

Chapter 10

THE MEAN GREEN PINE THING STRIKES AGAIN!

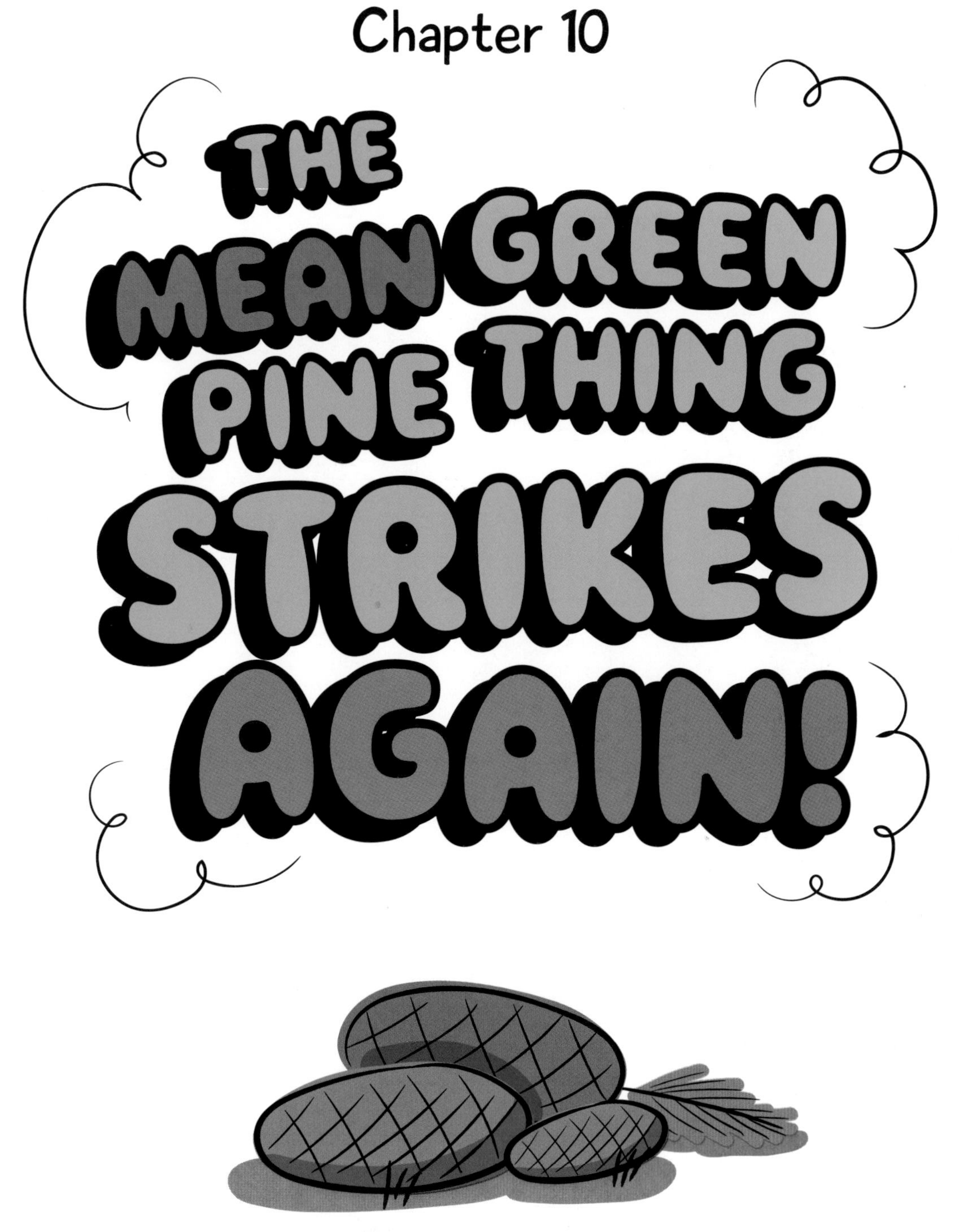

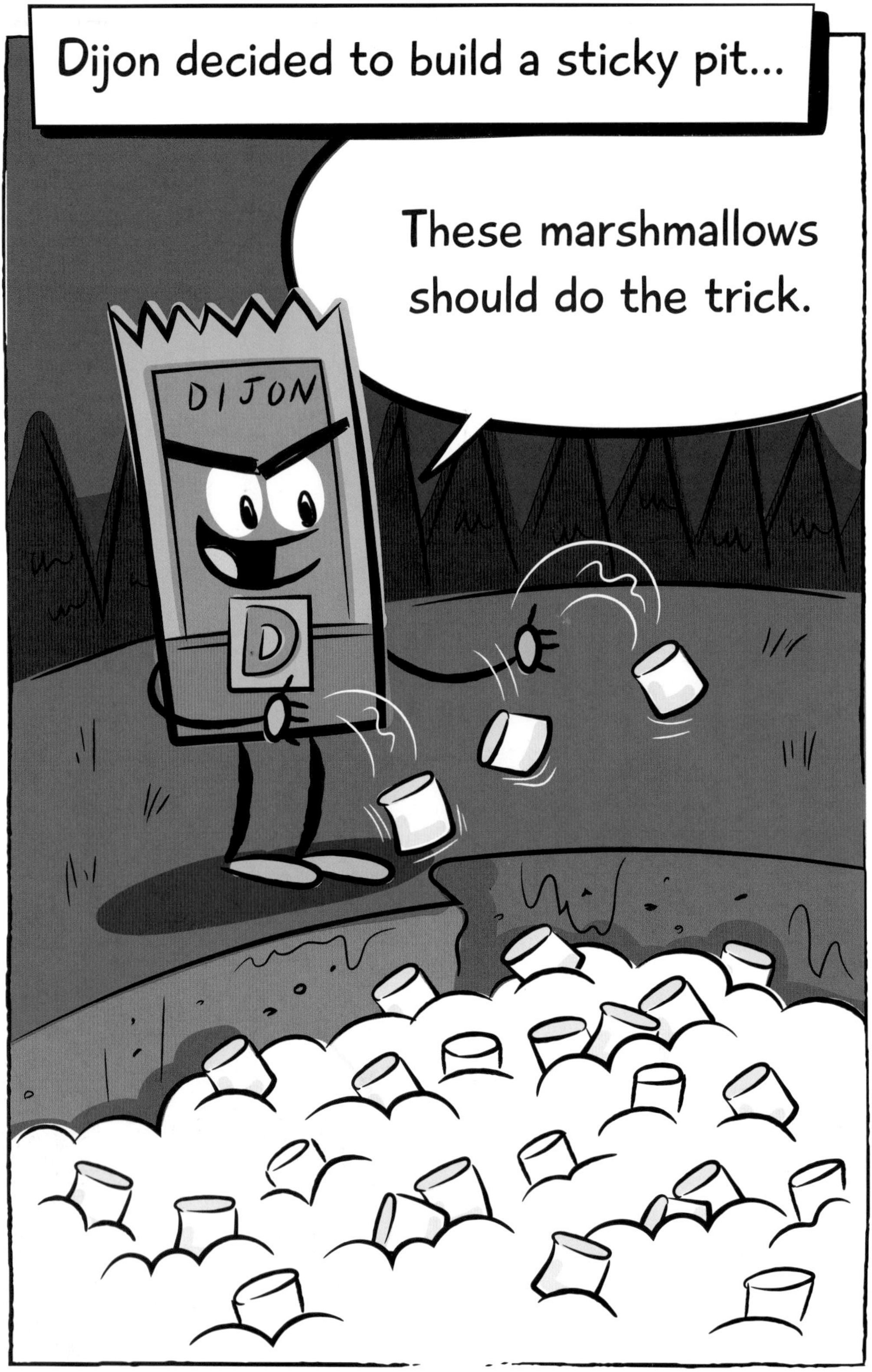
Dijon decided to build a sticky pit...
These marshmallows should do the trick.
DIJON
D

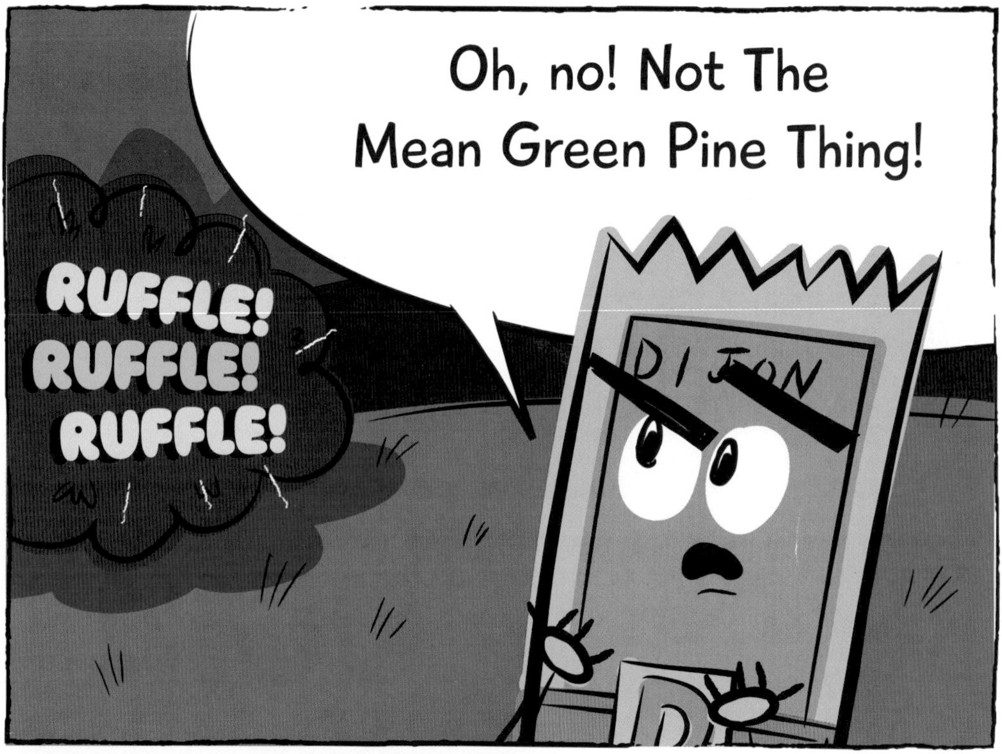
Oh, no! Not The Mean Green Pine Thing!
RUFFLE! RUFFLE! RUFFLE!
DIJON

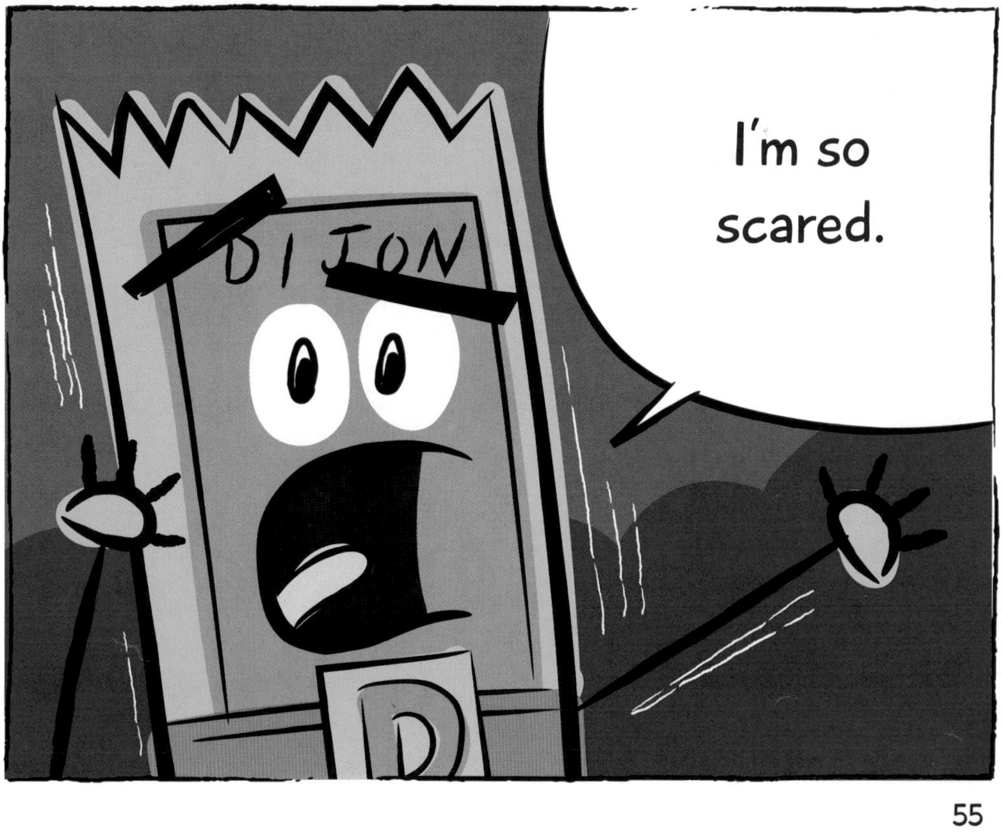
I'm so scared.
DIJON

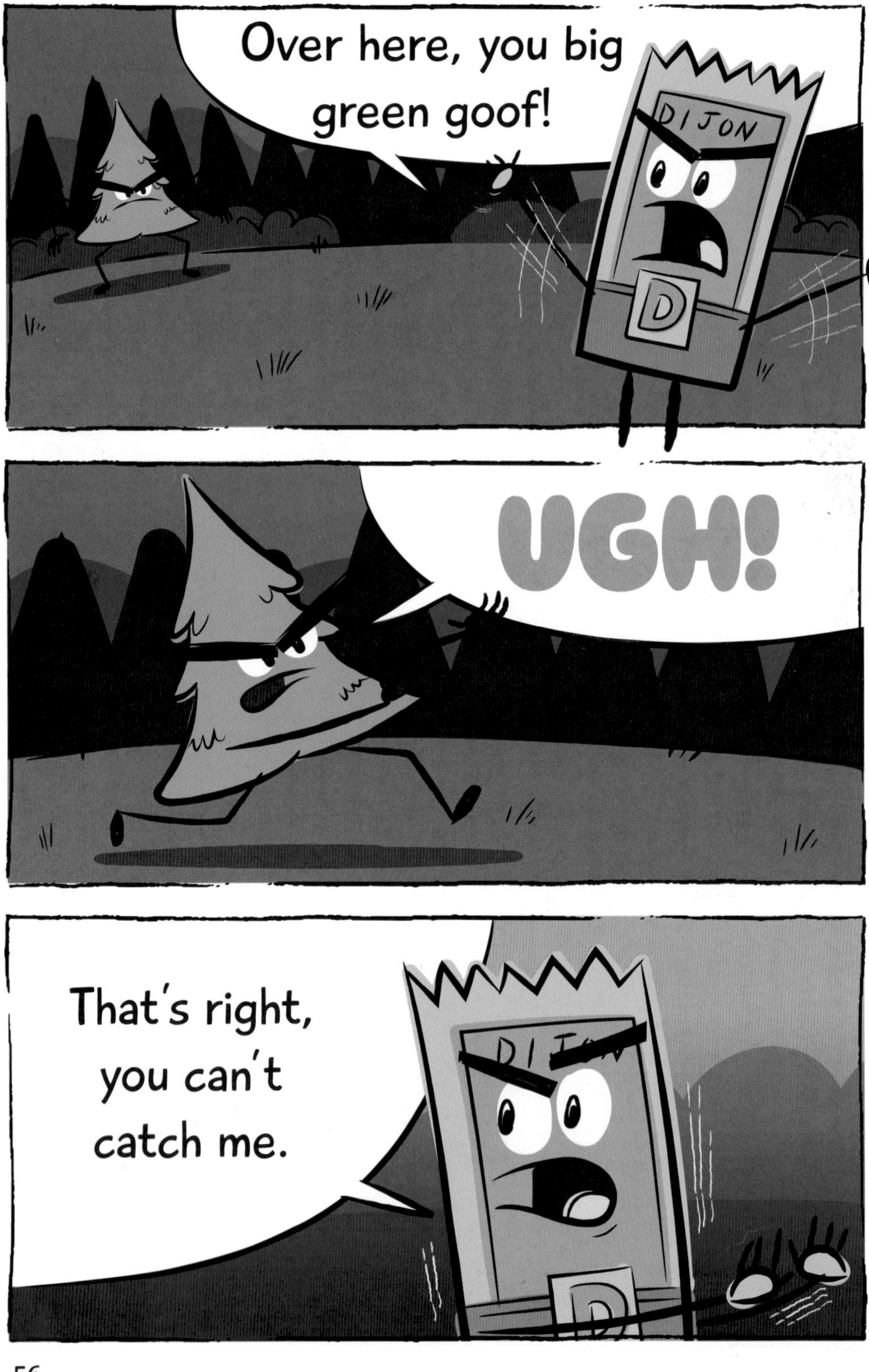
Over here, you big green goof!
DIJON
D
UGH!
That's right, you can't catch me.
DIJON
D

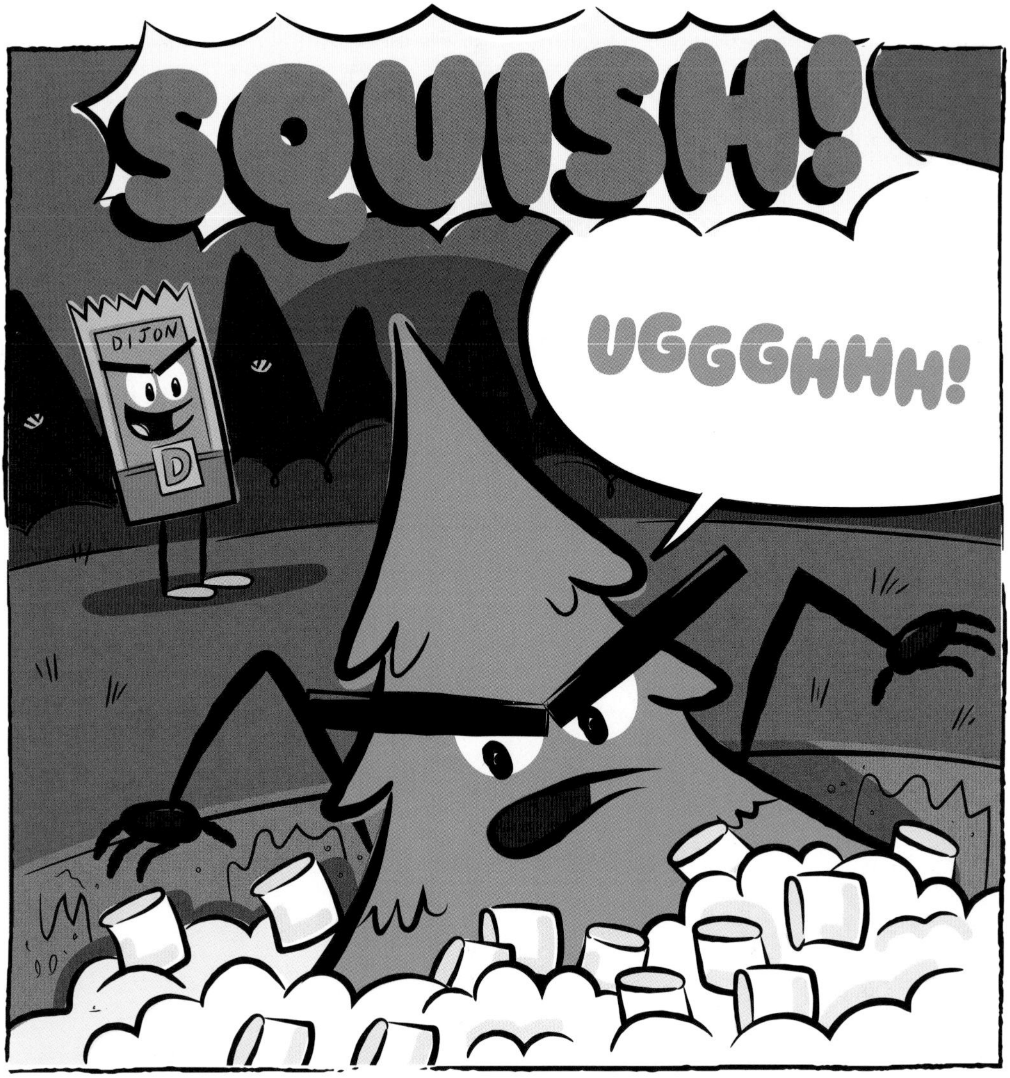
SQUISH!
DIJON
D
UGGGHHHH!

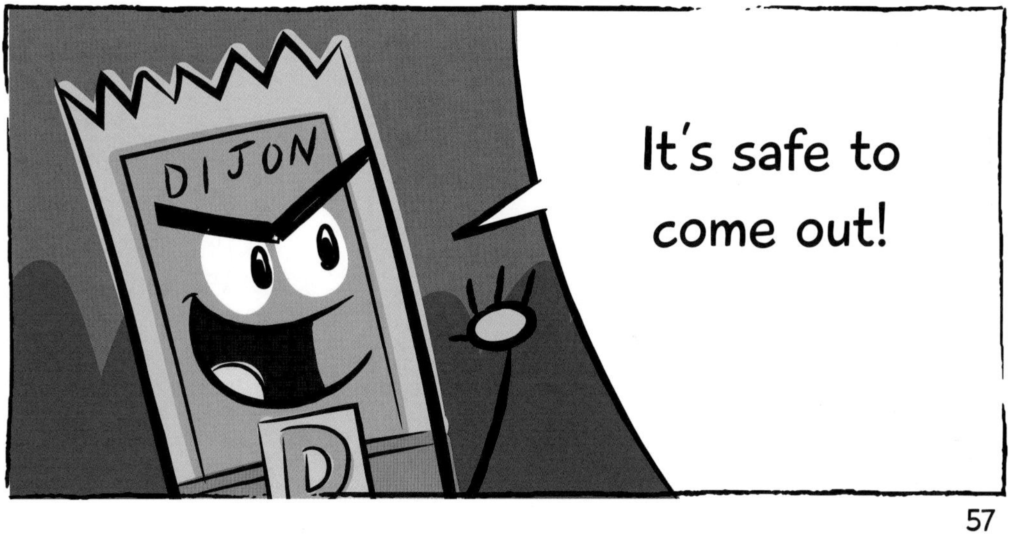
DIJON
D
It's safe to come out!

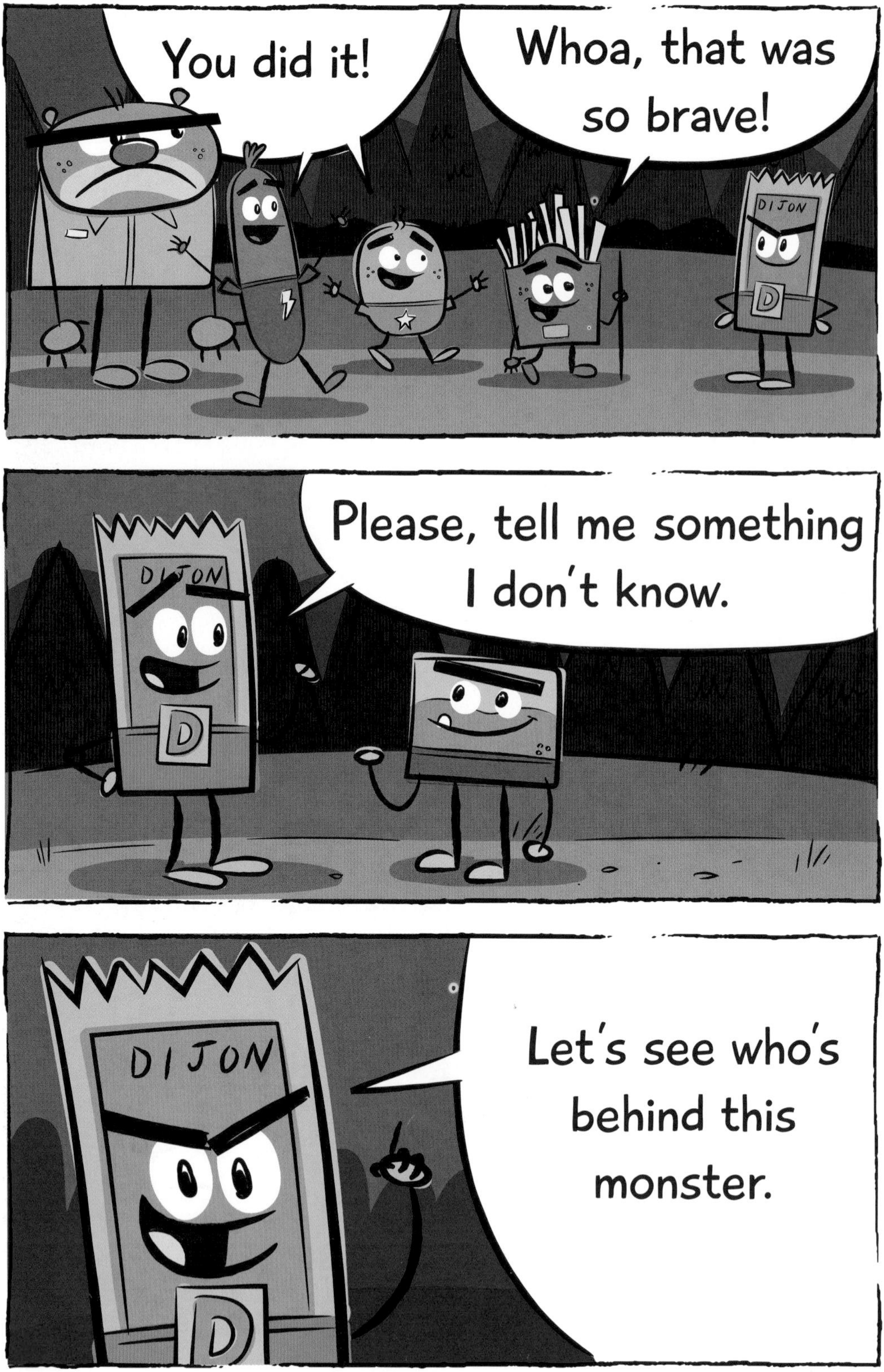
You did it!
Whoa, that was so brave!
DIJON
Please, tell me something I don't know.
DIJON
DIJON
Let's see who's behind this monster.

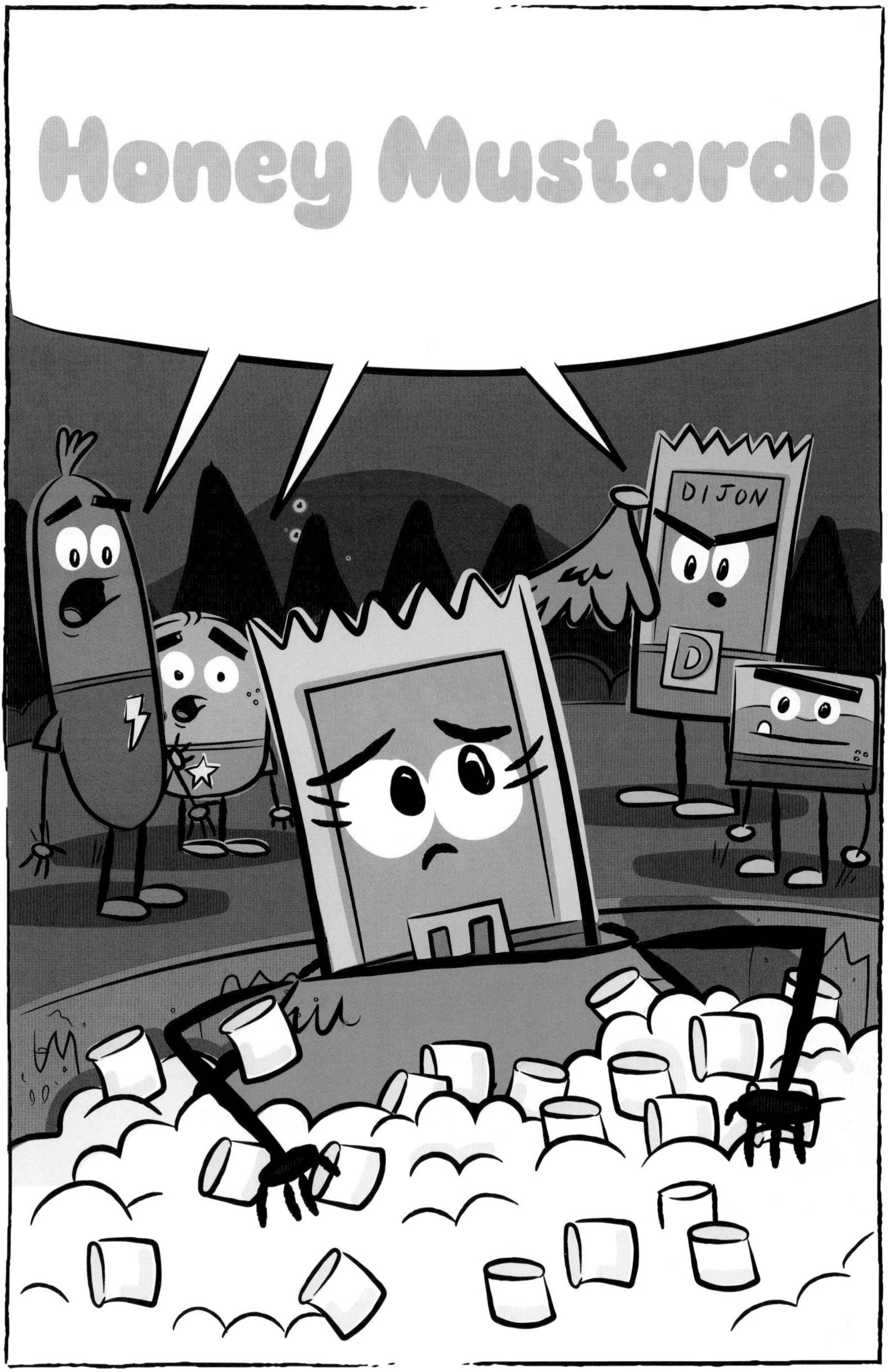
Honey Mustard!
DIJON
D

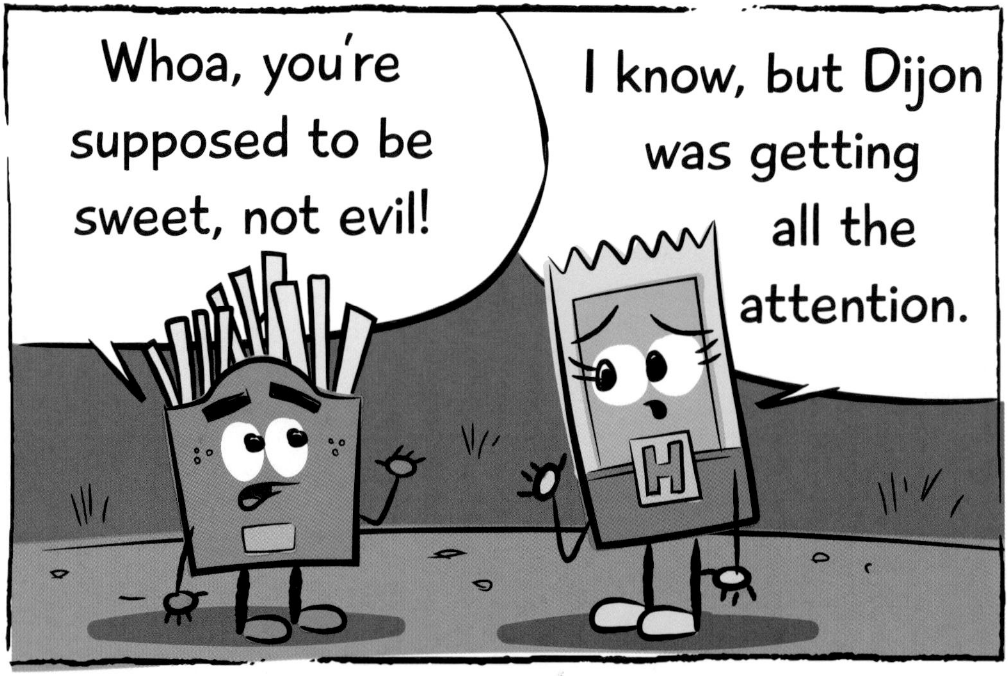
Whoa, you're supposed to be sweet, not evil!
I know, but Dijon was getting all the attention.

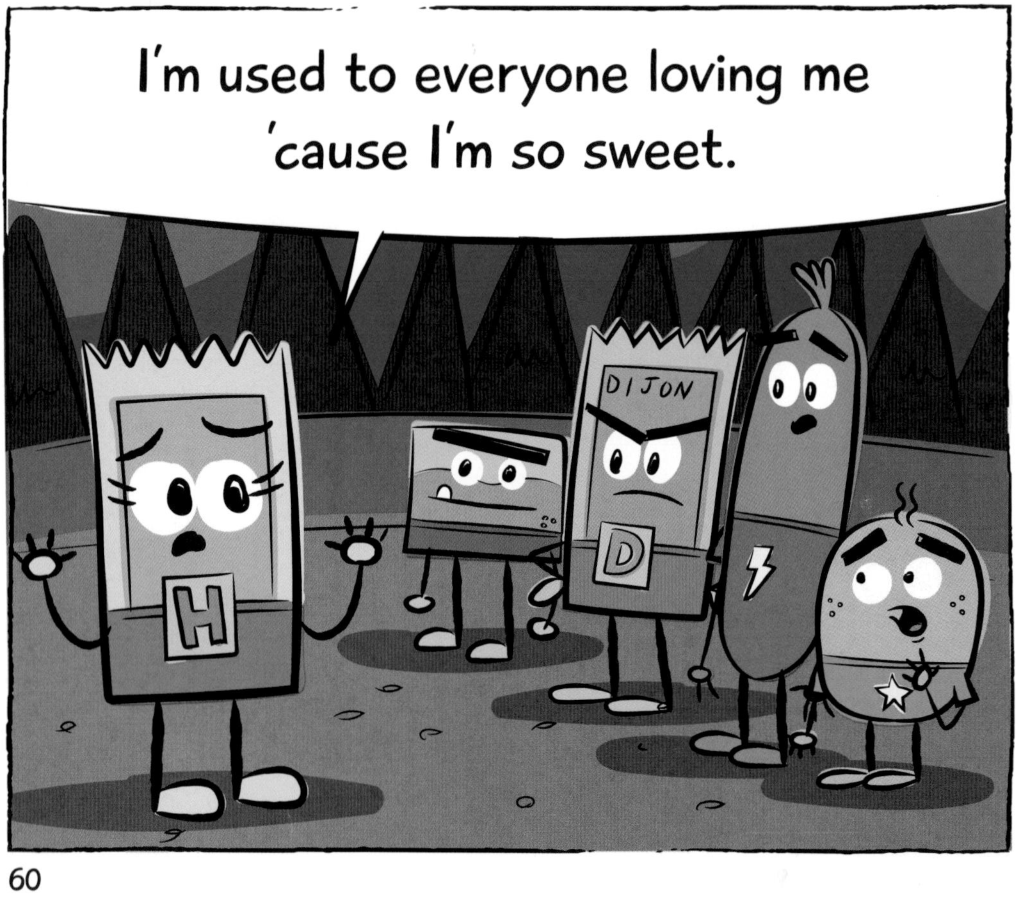
I'm used to everyone loving me 'cause I'm so sweet.
DIJON
H
D

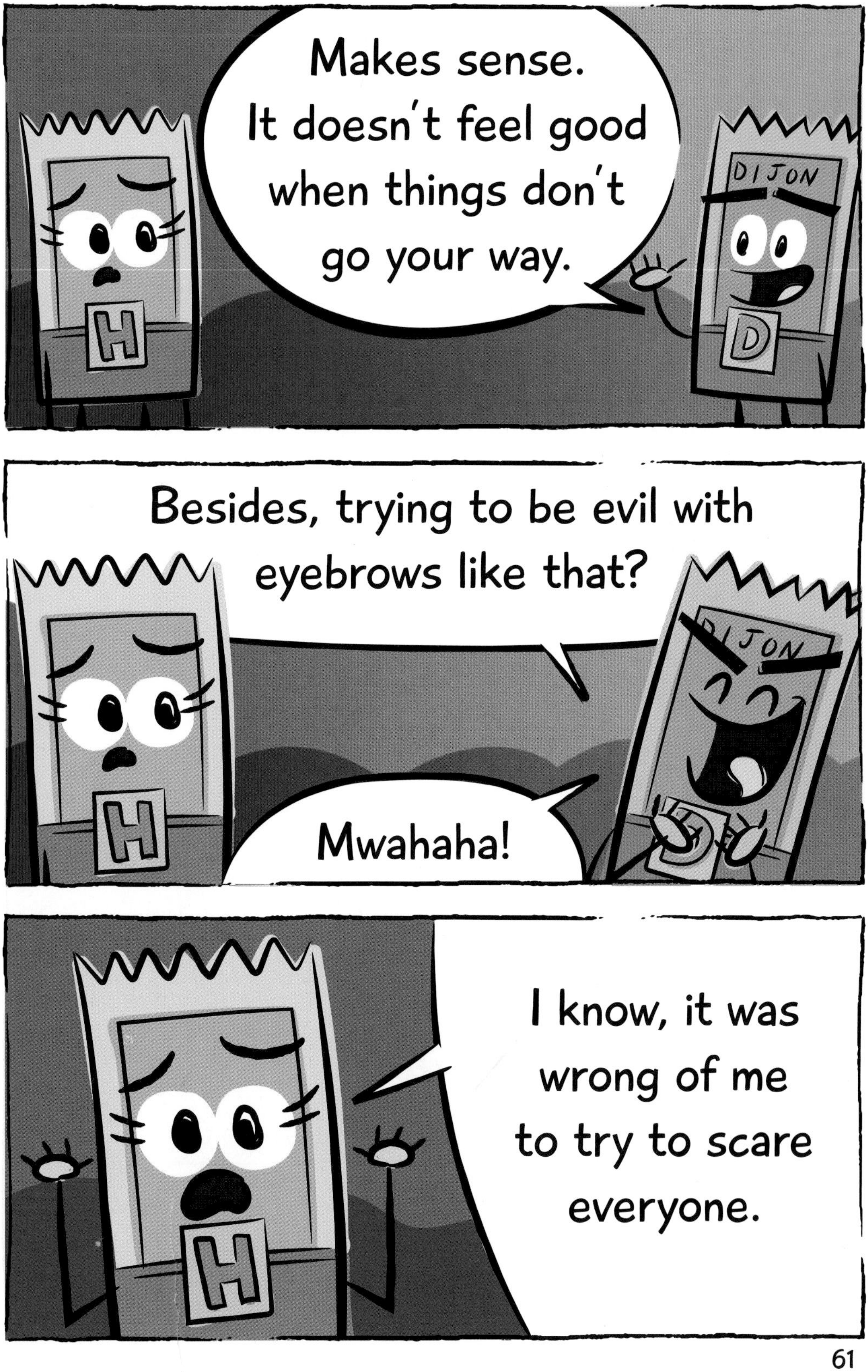
DIJON
Makes sense.
It doesn't feel good
when things don't
go your way.
Besides, trying to be evil with
eyebrows like that?
DIJON
Mwahaha!
I know, it was
wrong of me
to try to scare
everyone.

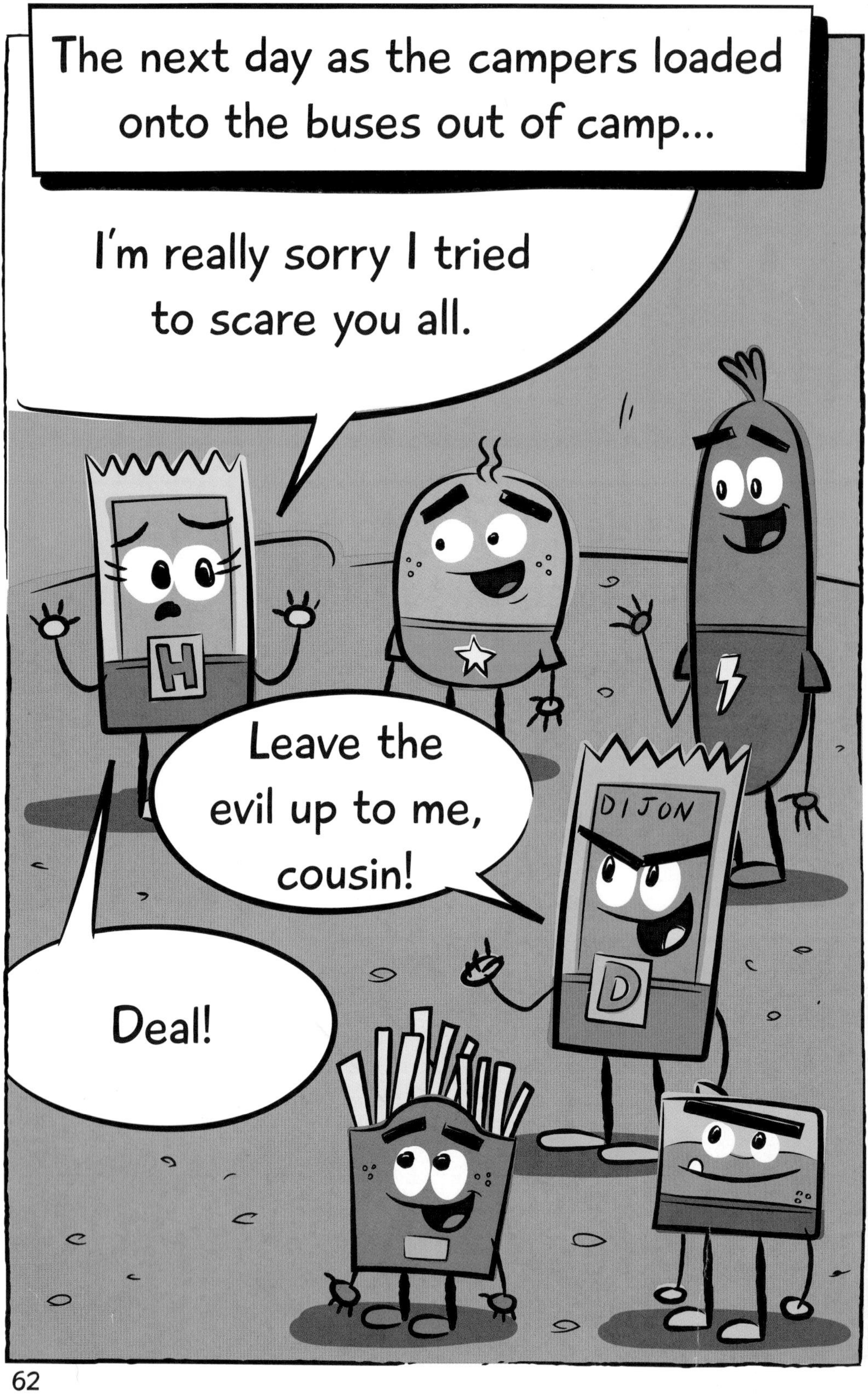
The next day as the campers loaded onto the buses out of camp...
I'm really sorry I tried to scare you all.
Leave the evil up to me, cousin!
DIJON
Deal!

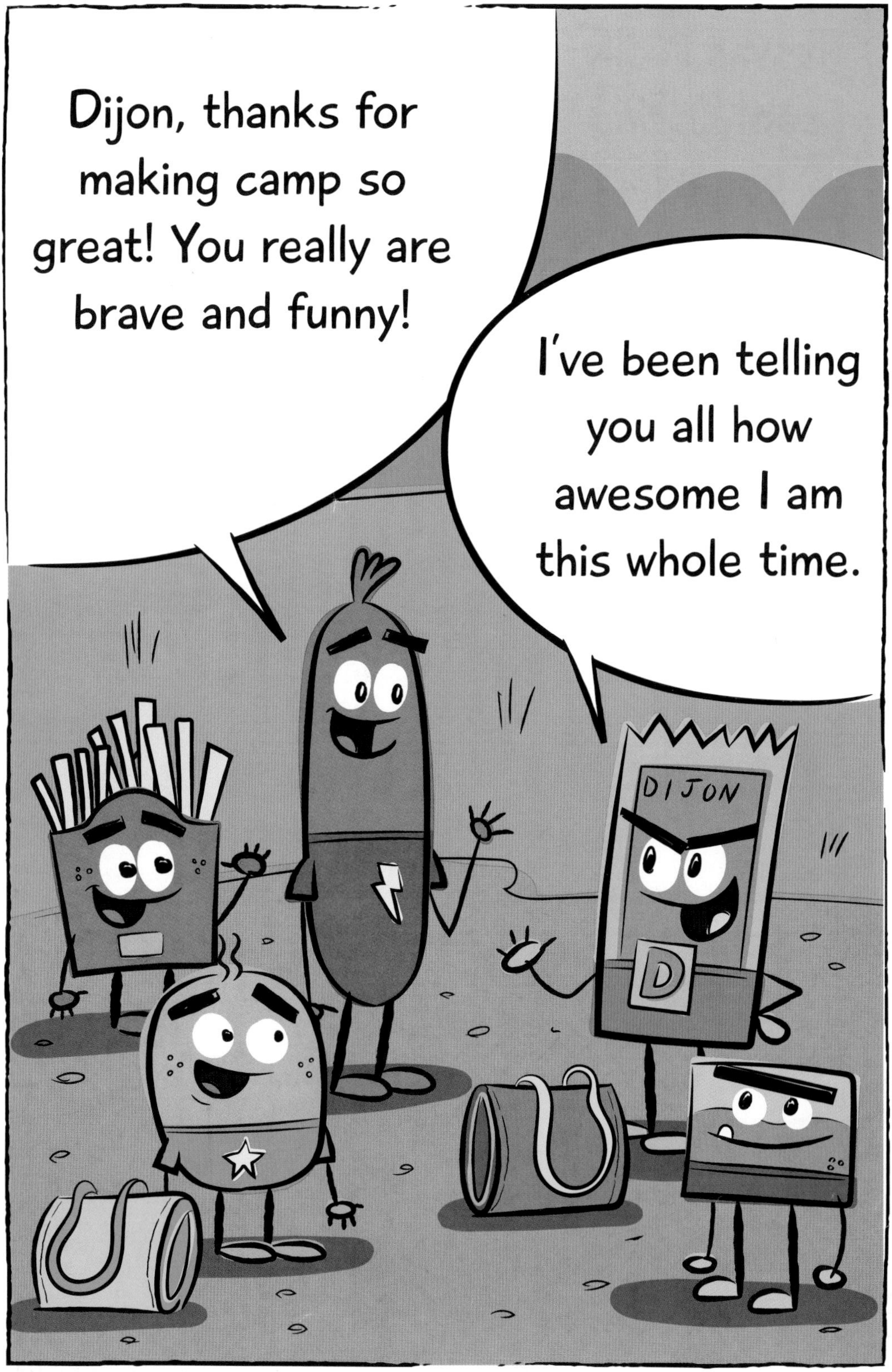
Dijon, thanks for making camp so great! You really are brave and funny!
I've been telling you all how awesome I am this whole time.
DIJON
D

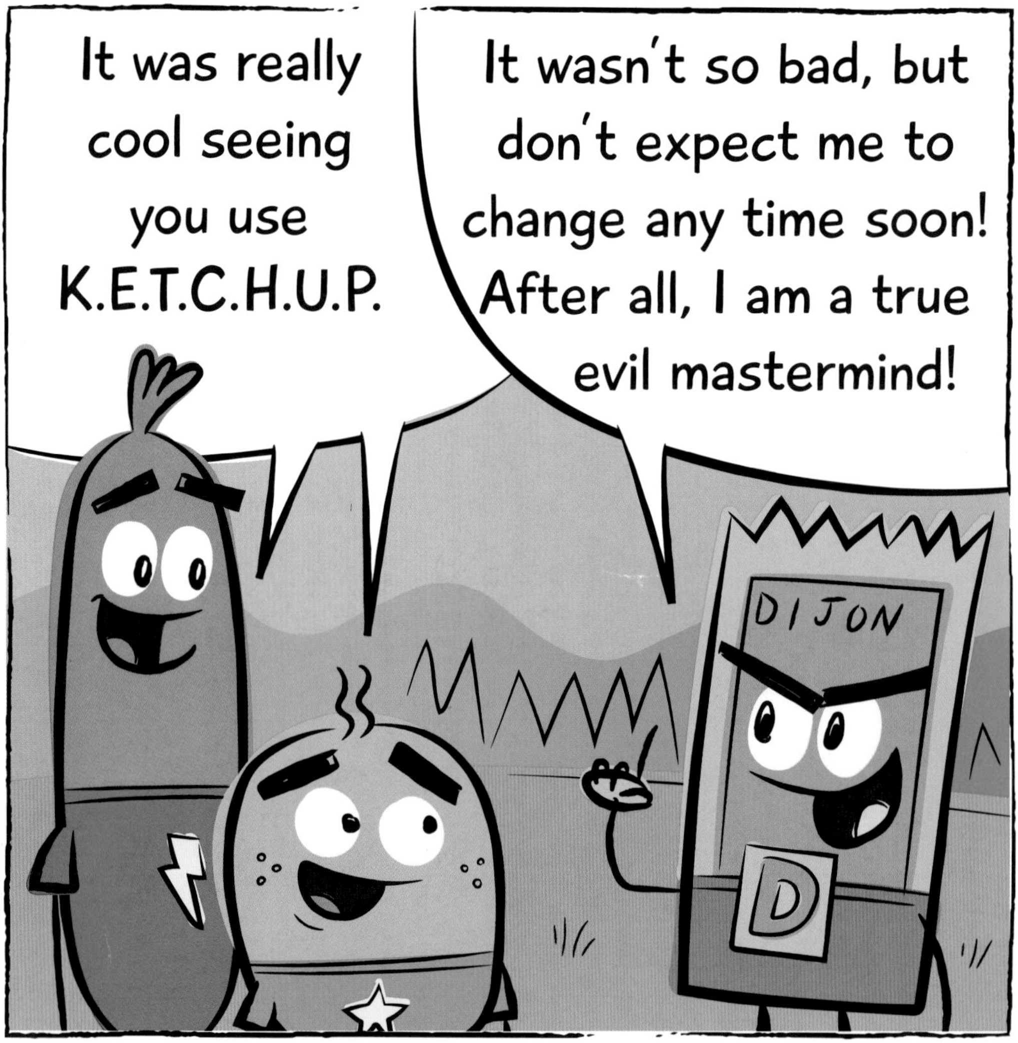
It was really cool seeing you use K.E.T.C.H.U.P.
It wasn't so bad, but don't expect me to change any time soon! After all, I am a true evil mastermind!
DIJON
D

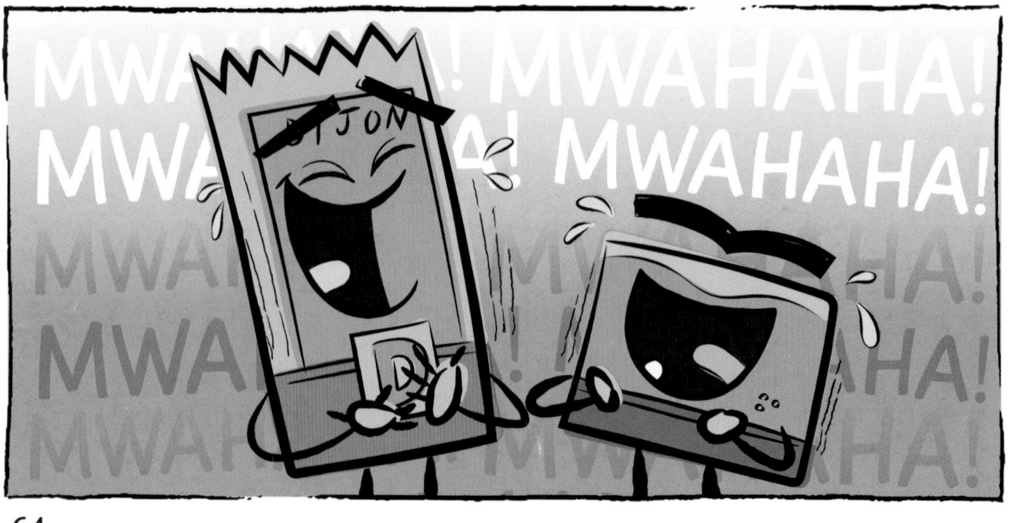
MWAHAHA! MWAHAHA!
MWAHAHA! MWAHAHA!
DIJON
D